Cornish Killing

A Sanford 3rd Age Club Mystery (#18)

David W Robinson

www.darkstroke.com

Copyright © 2019 by David W Robinson
Cover Image: Adobe Stock © DiViArts
Design by soqoqo
All rights reserved.

No part of this book may be used or reproduced in any manner whatsoever without written permission of the author or Crooked Cat Books except for brief quotations used for promotion or in reviews. This is a work of fiction. Names, characters, and incidents are used fictitiously.

First Dark Edition, darkstroke. 2019

Discover us online:
www.darkstroke.com

Find us on instagram:
www.instagram.com/darkstrokebooks

Include **#darkstroke** in a photo of yourself
holding his book on Instagram and
something nice will happen.

About the Author

David Robinson is a Yorkshireman now living in Manchester. Driven by a huge, cynical sense of humour, he's been a writer for over thirty years having begun with magazine articles before moving on to novels and TV scripts.

He has little to do with his life other than write, as a consequence of which his output is prodigious. Thankfully most of it is never seen by the great reading public of the world.

He has worked closely with Crooked Cat Books and darkstroke since 2012, when The Filey Connection, the very first Sanford 3rd Age Club Mystery, was published.

Describing himself as the Doyen of Domestic Disasters he can be found blogging at **www.dwrob.com** and he appears frequently on video (written, produced and starring himself) dispensing his mocking humour at **www.youtube.com/user/Dwrob96/videos**

The STAC Mystery series:

#1 The Filey Connection
#2 The I-Spy Murders
#3 A Halloween Homicide
#4 A Murder for Christmas
#5 Murder at the Murder Mystery Weekend
#6 My Deadly Valentine
#7 The Chocolate Egg Murders
#8 The Summer Wedding Murder
#9 Costa del Murder
#10 Christmas Crackers
#11 Death in Distribution
#12 A Killing in the Family
#13 A Theatrical Murder
#14 Trial by Fire
#15 Peril in Palmanova
#16 The Squire's Lodge Murders
#17 Murder at the Treasure Hunt
#18 A Cornish Killing

A
Cornish
Killing
A Sanford 3rd Age Club Mystery (#18)

Chapter One

Charlie Curnow's smartphone was set to 'vibrate only' when text messages came in. He preferred it that way. The less people were aware of him and his business, the better he liked it. But there were those times when, despite his craving for privacy, his actions spelled out something in the offing. Times such as now, when he received the message, *RWYA* (ready when you are). After he read it, he downed his second whiskey in one gulp, popped the glass back on the bar, and slid from his stool.

"Idle hands and the devil making work and all that," he said to the barman, and made his way unsteadily to the exit, followed by a muttered, "Drunken old sod," from behind the bar.

Once outside, the fresh air stabilised Charlie slightly. He told himself that it was the close confines of the pub which made him woozy.

He crossed the road zigzagging through a queue of Saturday afternoon traffic, and meandered through the rows of cars in the long stay car park by the harbour.

The summer season was all but over, and yet there were plenty of tourists on the harbour side, snapping away at the open (albeit distant) view of St Michael's Mount. It held no interest for Charlie. He had lived in Cornwall for almost twenty years and he'd seen it so many times that it failed to even register on his dimmed consciousness.

There was a time, not too long ago, when Charlie Curnow was a household name, frequently seen on TV as a stand-up comic and balladeer of the old-fashioned variety. The coming of observational comedy sank him, reduced him to the thankless role of entertainments manager at Gittings Caravan Park in Hayle. If it was beneath him (in his opinion) at least it kept a roof over his head and enough money coming in to keep him in booze and baccy. His wit was not fast or sharp enough for the pace of modern comedy, and the kind of ballads he sang were turned out *ad nauseum* by the current crop of boy bands.

It was a depressing scenario, and the prospects for the future were not good. At the age of 59, he had at least eight years to his state pension – assuming the government didn't move the goalposts again in the meantime – but that would literally be a pittance. He'd been self-employed ever since he came out of the army. In other words, for most of the last thirty-five years, and with his typical lack of regard for forward thinking, he had never taken out a pension plan. His ex-wife had made off with most of their joint savings leaving him with the sad thought that retirement, giving it all up to enjoy a life of leisure, would never come, or if it did, it would be hand in glove with the Grim Reaper.

But if he was strictly small time, there were compensations, and some of them were in the cartons currently filling the boot of his ageing Renault Clio.

Like most things in Charlie's life, the car was a clapped-out piece of junk. It had come off the production line sixteen years ago and it was beginning to show its age. The engine ran sweetly enough, but suffered the occasional miss, and according to a mechanic pal, it needed a new ignition coil. The central locking gave up the ghost long ago and because the only exterior lock was on the passenger door, it meant that had to be opened first, and Charlie had to lean in and press a dashboard switch to unlock the boot and driver's door. When it came to appearance, matters were just as bad. Charlie didn't know who owned the car before him but he/she had left it standing too long in the sun, and the paintwork was faded and peeling in places, allowing spots of rust to show through the dull silver-grey of the bodywork. Finally, only two of the four plastic wheel trims remained in place. The others had been missing for some time. Charlie had disposed of one in a dustbin on Gittings Holiday Park, and the other had worked loose and gone flying off during a journey to Newquay the previous winter. Fierce gales, heavy rain and an excess of whiskey ensured that Charlie remained oblivious to its disappearance until he arrived in Newquay. He wasn't really bothered, but it did explain the reaction of other drivers who had overtaken and remonstrated with him.

Despite the car's problems, amongst which Charlie also numbered an overflowing ashtray which, for the life of him, he could not detach and empty, the Renault suited his purposes. It got him from A to B, and it did not attract attention. Why should it? It was, after all, taxed, insured, and had a valid MOT certificate. When driving, Charlie stuck to the speed limits. Admittedly, it was more to do with conserving fuel and keeping down his expenses than any consideration for the law, but once again it helped him remain unobtrusive whilst on the road.

And such comparative anonymity was useful to him. During his frequent journeys to Penzance, the last thing he wanted was some nosy-parker cop asking him to open the boot.

The doors were already unlocked. Charlie climbed behind the wheel, slotted the ignition key home, and switched it on to open the electric windows.

In the passenger seat, Flick Tolley (who preferred the assumed Christian name to his real one, Frederick) jammed a hand-rolled cigarette into his mouth, retrieved a disposable lighter from the breast pocket of a short-sleeved shirt, and cupping his hands around the flame, lit up.

Charlie followed suit, and blew a cloud of smoke out through the open window. "Any problems?"

"Nope. But like you said, the price has gone up." Tolley's Cornish accent cut a fine contrast with Charlie's West Midlands' brogue, almost as if the two were from different countries.

Charlie tutted impatiently. "How much this time?"

Tolley held up four fingers of his right hand. "Four. And that don't include my commission."

Charlie dug out his wallet, and cast a sceptical eye on Tolley's smoke. "You're sure you haven't taken some of your commission already?"

"Come on, Charlie, I've been doing this long enough for you to know that I don't do that kind of thing. Check the cartons if you don't believe me. I haven't opened even one of 'em."

Charlie took a wad of twenty-pound notes from his wallet, counted them out, put a few back, and then counted them again, and added a tenner to them. "There you go, sunshine. Four and a half, all up. Tell your mate three weeks. In the meantime get onto your contact in Falmouth, and tell him next week."

Jamming the money into his hip pocket, preparing to leave the car, Tolley raised his eyebrows. "Next week? Bit soon, innit?"

Charlie tapped the side of his bulbous nose. "That's why I'm the wheeler-dealer and you're the gofer. We've a big party coming from up north this week. Some place called Sanford, in Yorkshire, and you know what those Yorkies are like for a good deal." He jerked a thumb back towards the boot. "With luck and a following wind, I'll shift most of that this week." He checked the time. "Almost three o'clock. You'd better get back to Gittings. I'll give it a quarter of an hour and follow you."

Tolley climbed out of the car. "Roger, dodger. Catch you later."

***

From one of the panoramic windows of the Waterside Shopping Centre, Wynette Kalinowski trained a pair of field glasses on the vista below and ahead of her. She was not studying the view of St Michael's Mount. Instead her glasses were concentrated on the long-stay car park.

It was as she suspected. The joint absence of her immediate boss, Charlie Curnow, and Flick Tolley occurred too often for it to be coincidence. It was always on a Saturday (changeover day, and the slackest time of the week on any holiday park, not just Gittings) and they always contrived to arrive back at the park within fifteen minutes of each other.

An adequate singer and dancer, this was her third season at Gittings, and she had begun to despair of the big time. She had hoped that the experience of working on a holiday park would be enough to get the attention of an agent. She'd certainly sent out enough queries and showreels, but there were no takers, and she came to the sad conclusion that she would remain one of life's also-rans, putting on turns in clubs and pubs throughout the lower end of the Cornish peninsula.

That being the case, she wanted something more from Flick than the occasional romp in his or her bed, and what she had just seen might just be the angle she needed.

Satisfied with her observations, she tucked the small glasses in her bag, and made her way back towards the escalators. She was on duty at six, she had bingo to call at half past eight, and a forty-five minutes song and dance spot at nine fifteen. Time, tide, and Gittings waited for no man… or woman.

Chapter Two

The dagger flew through the air. Joe dropped to the floor and rolled away. The glistening, steel blade whistled past him and embedded itself in the wooden jamb of the kitchen doorway.

As the murderous Snettitsky rushed him, Joe flipped onto his back and kicked out, his right leg flying straight up to catch the KGB agent squarely on the jaw. The Russian staggered back, Joe leapt to his feet, crouched and rammed his bone-hard skull into Snettitsky's abdomen. It was like head-butting a block of concrete. He needed something sharper.

He stretched for the knife, still embedded in the door jamb, but Snettitsky grabbed him by the shoulders and hurled him across the café.

Joe tumbled over table 5, where the *Daily Express* lay open at the crossword page, now stained with spilled coffee. Crashing from the table to the floor, he rolled expertly to his feet, and as Snettitsky rushed him he lashed out with a side of his hand to the Russian's throat. Snettitsky gagged and Joe leapt upon his back, wrapping his arms around the thick, muscular neck.

Snettitsky staggered around the floor, crashing Joe's back into the soft drinks cabinet, the bare wall, and the glass front door, which shook in protest.

Joe's grip loosened and Snettitsky shrugged him off. As the giant Russian turned to attack, Joe rushed towards the kitchen and the array of chef's knives hanging on the wall.

Snettitsky intercepted him, and cast him to one side behind the counter. Joe's head connected with the overhead shelf, rattling cups, saucers, beakers and dinner plates. Joe grabbed the handle of the large metal teapot he used for serving customers, and hurled it at Snettitsky. The Russian brought his arms up and as the teapot connected with his forearm, he brushed it aside, and it flew across the café, bouncing on a couple of tables before crashing to the tiled floor by the windows.

They half crouched in the cramped confines of the rear of the counter, both of them ready to make the next move, ready to parry the next move.

Joe leapt, his hands making for Snettitsky's throat. The Russian sidestepped, caught Joe, turned him, and held him in an unbreakable headlock, his powerful arm coming around Joe's neck and squeezing.

"The secret, Mr Joe. Now."

"I'll see you in hell first." Joe's voice was a rasping squawk.

"Then you take it to your grave." The KGB man was out of breath. He had obviously never come across an opponent as tough as Joe.

As he spoke, he reached to his wristwatch, unclipped the winder and slid it out, exposing a long sliver of steel which gleamed in the overhead, halogen lighting. It came about Joe's neck, and Snettitsky pulled with all his strength.

Joe's eyes watered as his airway began to shut down. He had to do something quickly or face eternity. The knives he so desperately wanted were out of reach, and the only thing close enough was the chiller, just ahead of him. He reached a hand towards it. He was short by four inches. What was it he had thought when he head-butted Snettitsky? He needed something sharper? He jabbed a hard elbow back into Snettitsky's lower gut, and this time, he heard the Russian gasp in pain. Snettitsky's grip slackened perceptibly. Joe pulled forward and the steel choker bit into the skin of his neck. Determined that this would not be the end, he reached shaking fingers into the chiller and grabbed the first thing he could.

With a swift movement, he jerked his open palm over his left shoulder and rammed the stale, lemon meringue tart into the Russian's face.

With a grunt of protest, Snettitsky's grip loosened, Joe spun him and wrapped the steel line around the stout throat. He pulled with all his might and Snettitsky began to gag.

Triumph burned in Joe's voice. "Nobody, but nobody gets the secret of my steak and kidney pudding. And you, Snettitsky, exit here…"

Exit here… Exit here… Exit here…

***

"Exeter."

The sound of Keith Lowry's voice woke Joe Murray from his vivid dream, and he took a moment to orientate himself.

Alongside him, Brenda Jump was immersed in the brochure for their ultimate destination, Gittings Holiday Park, near Hayle. Her MP3 player was plugged into her ears and she remained oblivious to everything around her, including Keith's announcement.

A copy of Ian Fleming's *From Russia With Love* lay face down on Joe's lap. He had spent most of the six-hour journey from Sanford reading it, and the last thing he could remember was seeing the exit for Weston-super-Mare an hour and however many miles back. He only noticed that because the 3rd Age Club had once spent an Easter weekend there.

Keith slowed down and moved into the inside lane, ready for leaving the M5. He was due for a forty-five minute break as required by law. He'd already taken one such break on the outskirts of Knutsford in Cheshire, less than two hours after they left Sanford.

"You have to plan these things, Joe," he had explained at the time. "If I push on as far as I can now, I'd probably get to, say, Gloucester, and then I'd need a second break in a layby on the A30… In other words, in the middle of nowhere, and your moaning old gits would be whining that they need a cup of tea and the toilet. It's better to take a break at Knutsford and then Exeter."

Joe accepted the explanation without argument, but he was not out of questions. "And how long from Exeter?"

Keith pursed his lips in a supposed display of experience and intelligence. "A hundred miles... Say, two hours and change."

As Keith pulled off the motorway, and made his way round to the service area, Joe checked his watch. A few minutes past one. It would be two o'clock before they left Exeter, which meant it would be getting on for half past four when they arrived at the holiday park. Not for the first time, he questioned the sanity of booking a week in Cornwall.

It was an unusual excursion for the 3rd Age Club. Usually, they went away only for weekends, but the distance involved (getting on for 400 miles) tempted the members to plump for a full week.

And this time, Sheila was not with them. She was still on honeymoon in the Cape Verde Islands. Joe envied her. Notwithstanding the nine-hour journey, he relished the prospect of a week in Cornwall, but he would still prefer the tropical sunshine of Boa Vista.

Like Joe, Brenda would miss her best friend, and Sheila's marriage had prompted some changes. Joe had originally planned to share a caravan with his intermittent lady friend, Maddy Chester, but as a small-time TV personality, she had broadcasting commitments she could not get out of and, as a result, she had to forego the dubious pleasure of a week's holiday with him (dubious because she preferred the sunny beaches of the Mediterranean to southwest England). Brenda, who would normally share with Sheila, suggested that she and Joe should share, with Brenda taking the double bedroom, and Joe sleeping in the twin, and he agreed.

"I just hope I don't cramp your style," he had said to her.

Brenda had responded with a customary smirk. "I'll lock you out while I'm done with the lucky man."

And Joe remembered thinking that he wouldn't put it past her. "And what happens if I hit it off?" he had demanded.

Brenda's reply came with a speed that said she had anticipated the objection. "You can go back to her place."

Keith pulled the bus into the car park, killed the engine and took down his microphone. "Okay, folks, this is Exeter services. We'll be here for at least three quarters of an hour. It's just turned one, so let's say you need to be back on the bus for quarter to two."

Joe, ever alert to the speed at which some of the more elderly club members did not move, jumped out of his seat, and as Keith opened the door, he left the bus and waited for Brenda. When she joined him, they walked side-by-side to the cafeteria.

The last week of September had seen a fine, Indian summer settle over most of the country. It seemed to Joe that West Yorkshire in general and Sanford in particular were the exceptions. When they boarded the bus on the car park of the Miner's Arms at half past six in the morning, it was under the malign shroud of a fine drizzle, adding to the autumn chill biting into his fingers, and Joe was thankful that he was no longer Chair of the 3rd Age Club. Having yielded the position to Les Tanner, it was now the Captain's task to check everyone on board, and when Joe left his small suitcase with Keith, he was able to settle into his seat alongside Brenda, and take advantage of the rising warmth inside the coach.

An hour later, by which time they were dropping down the steep hill on the M62 into Greater Manchester, he was dry and comfortable, and by then, Brenda was sleeping.

It was an uneventful journey. Tedious would be Joe's description, and he was grateful for the machinations of Mr Fleming's imaginative espionage tale. Joe had read the book many times, and it remained one of his favourites, but even so, by the time they reached Birmingham, about three and a quarter hours after leaving Sanford, the delights of Roseland on the Black Sea coast, the Istanbul bazaar, Zagreb and Paris had begun to fade. He spent the next hour, between Birmingham and Bristol, working through the crossword in the Daily Express, and then returned to the Bond novel.

Little wonder that he soon nodded off and dreamt of confrontation with the cold-blooded killer from *Smersh*. But how did his agile subconscious come to replace the villain's name with a variation on that of Sid Snetterton? True, Sid was a competitor in Sanford, but he managed a snack bar near the town centre and it bore no comparison to The Lazy Luncheonette. Everyone, from the mechanics at Broadbent Autos to the draymen of Sanford Brewery said so.

While visiting the toilets in the services, he decided that the dream was symptomatic of his professional paranoia (he had always been fiercely proud of his homemade steak and kidney pudding) and the singular lack of excitement in his life.

Once in the cafeteria, he and Brenda secured sandwiches and coffee at the counter, and sat at a window table, where he told her of the dream and his conclusions.

"Excitement?" Brenda cried. "Joe, you've solved more murders than Scotland Yard."

"That's not what I mean. I mean *real* excitement."

Brenda scowled. "I should have thought you'd had enough of that with the business in Palmanova."

Joe shuddered at the memory of a series of attacks which could have cost him his life. "Yeah, but I always pictured myself as a man of action."

"You are. Especially when you're serving the draymen at breakfast."

"That's not the kind of action I had in mind."

With a sigh, Brenda bit into a cheese and salad sandwich, chewed vigorously and swallowed, washing it down with a mouthful of coffee. "What kind of an action man would you make? You stand five foot five—"

"Five foot six."

"Only when you're wearing thick-soled trainers." She paused to let the riposte strike home. "You're one of life's shortarses, Joe, and you're a cook. Yours is a licence to grill not kill." She glanced through the windows at the balmy, September sunshine, and deliberately changed the subject. "It looks like we're going to have a good week, weather-wise, at least."

Joe yawned, then bit off a lump of his tuna and mayonnaise sandwich, chewed and swallowed it. His neutral features turned to a grimace. "It beats me how the food in these places can be so consistent. It's rubbish, and it doesn't matter where you stop, anywhere in the country, it's the same rubbish."

Brenda did not agree. "It's not bad, Joe. A bit pricey, but it's like airline food, isn't it? A consequence of mass catering. Console yourself with the thought that if you were on one of these reality shows, you'd beat their cooks hands down." She, too, took another bite of her sandwich. "I wonder how Sheila's getting on. It's strange going away without her."

"I suppose we'll have to get used to it." Joe chuckled. "She'll be all right, topping up her tan and getting used to sleeping in a double bed again. I hope she's had more than a view of the bedroom ceiling."

Brenda could not resist a giggle at the innuendo. "She's not like that, and you know it."

"Yes, but it's what honeymoons are all about, isn't it? I know. I've been on one."

Brenda ignored Joe's cynical tone at the memory of his ten-year marriage. "Lloret-de-mar, wasn't it?"

Joe nodded and drank from his cup again. "Alison caught a touch of Montezuma's revenge, and I spent the last half of the fortnight propping up the hotel bar on my own." He pushed the remains of his sandwich to one side and drank more coffee. Anything to take away the cardboard taste of the bread and its filling. "Anyway, by the time we get back from Cornwall, she'll be home, and I daresay we'll get all the gory details…" He cast a jocular eye on Brenda. "Well, you will. I'll only get the overview."

The cafeteria was filling up, mainly with the Sanford party of seventy people. They divided themselves up into standard cliques. Alec and Julia Staines sat with Les Tanner and his lady love, Sylvia Goodson, who gave Joe and Brenda an indulgent smile as she sat down. George Robson and Owen Frickley, workmates as well as co-members, joined Mort Norris and his wife, while Cyril Peck and Mavis Barker sat with the elderly Pyecocks, Irene and Norman. Some things, Joe reflected, never changed.

"Another couple of hours to our destination," Brenda said, bringing him back from his reverie.

"I hope it's worth the journey. You know anything about the place?"

Brenda shook her head. "Only what the brochure tells us. On-site restaurant, swimming pools, games area for the kids, and the show bar. Some of the activities are interesting, but they may not be on at this time of year. A climbing wall, for instance, and archery lessons. It's a bit late in the season for them."

"Archery?" Joe sneered. "What's that about? Home rule for Cornwall and be ready to ward off invading Devonians?"

"Sport, Joe, and by sport I mean different to elbow bending at the bar, chucking darts at a board, and seeing how many different women you can pull in a week."

Joe disregarded the reproof. He knew it was aimed not at him but men like George Robson and Owen Frickley. "You said there's a show bar, so how about evening entertainment?"

"According to the brochure, there's live entertainment every night. But again, with it being so late in the season, they don't get guest artists. It's put on by the camp's entertainment crew."

Joe snorted. "A shed load of wannabes screeching into the microphone prancing around the stage every night I suppose. And I'll bet there's bingo."

Brenda tittered. "You can't get away from bingo in places like Benidorm, so you have no chance in Cornwall."

Soon, with the forty-five minute break coming to an end, Les Tanner circulated amongst the members, reminding them that they were due back on the bus, and they should visit the toilets before boarding, because there would be no more stops. To Joe, it was pointless advice. To a man (and woman) the club members were all over fifty years of age (it was a requirement of membership), that time of life when the body's demands for regular relief tended to forceful reminders.

Ten minutes later, he was back in his seat, and picked up Fleming's novel once again, and as Keith pulled out of the service area, turning south onto the motorway, he settled into the devilish plot to eliminate James Bond.

Ten miles further along, at that point where the Devon Expressway parted company with the A380 for Torbay, his eyes began to droop, and long before they reached Plymouth, he was sound asleep.

Chapter Three

On arrival at Gittings, Joe was off the bus with the same speed he had deployed at Exeter Services, this time right behind Keith, just ahead of Brenda, but while their driver began to unload the luggage, Joe and Brenda stood by the door to assist the more elderly members, such as Irene Pyecock.

Gittings Holiday Park was a standard caravan park. A vast expanse of lawns and holiday homes, interspersed with gravel lanes, all carrying a warning of a 5mph on-site speed limit. The place stood on a hillside a couple of miles to the north of Hayle. From the car park, they could see nothing other than the interminable lines of caravans, but Joe knew that to the West, beyond the low, rolling hummock of grassland which blocked the view of the sea, was a wide, sandy beach, one of the largest in the country.

Immediately ahead of them was the reception centre, a free-standing building painted white, lending it an almost adobe appearance. Les Tanner made for the office the moment he got off the coach. Joe did not envy him. It had once been his task to book all members in, collect the keys and distribute them according to the hotel/holiday park's allocation list. If he knew anything about the British tourist industry, Tanner would be missing for at least forty minutes.

Attached to the nearby entertainment block was a snack bar, its panoramic windows overlooking the neat lawns and picnic area outside its doors. Once the luggage was unloaded, and Keith drove the bus away to the official parking area, most of the members made their way to the gaily decorated building and before long, they were settling in with cups of tea, coffee, soft drinks, sandwiches and cakes.

Preferring the fresh air to the interior of the cafeteria, Joe allowed Brenda to pick up two cups of tea before she joined him, George Robson and Owen Frickley at one of the outside tables. Joe savoured the mild sunshine of early autumn. His breathing difficulties, exacerbated since he began smoking again, could sometimes be overwhelming, especially in hot weather. He always found it easier to breathe in late September, early October.

"It'd be easier still if you packed the weed in for good," George commented.

"That's smart coming from you," Joe retorted. "But at least it's the only bad habit I have. You've got all the rest, including drinking too much and putting it about too much."

George grinned. "Yolo."

Joe frowned. "Yo-yo."

Brenda laughed and Owen, a wide grin crossing his rough features, almost choked on his tea

"Yolo, you berk," George corrected him. "You only live once."

Joe puffed contentedly on a hand-rolled cigarette and blowing out the smoke, pouted triumphantly at George. "You took the words right out of my mouth."

A middle-aged man and a much younger woman were making their way towards the nearby reception building. He stood about six feet but his height was offset by a large paunch. He wore shabby, beige trousers, the cuffs flapping above a pair of battered trainers. Above the waist (Joe considered the word in its loosest possible sense) beneath a scruffy, black fleece, he was clad in a ragged, tight-fitting, white shirt, urgently in need of a tour through a washing machine's full cycle, which did nothing to hide his massive beer belly. His hair had thinned to the point where it was non-existent on the crown but curled untidily over his collar. Even from a distance, his large nose shone a dull red, matching his cheeks, and Joe diagnosed boozer's blush.

The contrast between him and the young woman could not be more striking. She stood about five and a half feet, slim, curvaceous, her bosom accentuated by a close-fitting blouse and a clearly visible bra which pinched in and lifted up. Most of her legs showed below the hem of a body-hugging skirt. Her auburn hair was styled in a tasteful shower which Joe guessed must have cost a fortune at the hairdressers. Her ruby lips, which would probably be capable of the most alluring smile, were set stern, and her narrow, brown eyes focused on the man alongside and slightly ahead of her.

As they drew near, the conversation was plain for all to hear, especially when the man spoke.

"Listen to me, Winnie, either get on with the job or get out. I don't care which. Plenty more warblers where you come from."

She stopped, and he carried on towards Joe and his friends. Her voice followed him. "Remember what I know about you, Charlie Curnow."

Now he stopped, and turned to take her on, but she was already walking away, moving quickly across the gravel road towards the older caravans.

Charlie turned and beamed upon the four Sanford 3rd Age Club members. "Sorry about that. Can't get the staff, you know… Well, distaff." He chuckled at his weak joke, and strode towards them, offering his hand. "Charlie Curnow. Entertainments Manager."

Joe shook his hand first. "I'm Joe Murray. We're with the party from Yorkshire."

Charlie shook hands with them in turn, and waved an arm at the sunshine. "It looks like you've chosen the right week, and it's my job to make sure you enjoy it. You might remember me from television a few years ago. I used to do regular variety shows."

All four blanked him.

"I don't watch much telly," Joe said in an effort to cover the potentially embarrassing silence. He rapidly changed the subject. "I hope you have plenty in store for us this week."

"It's all in the brochure, Joe. The only thing we don't have is the archery." Charlie delivered another false laugh. "If the autumn wind gets up round here, you never know where the arrows will end up."

George got in first this time. "It's no problem, Charlie. We don't fancy ourselves as modern Robin Hoods, anyway."

"You do surprise me. What with Robin Hood being a Yorkshireman and all."

Joe crushed out his cigarette and shook his head. "No way was Robin Hood ever a Yorkshireman." He grinned at Charlie. "No self-respecting Yorkshireman would steal from the rich and give to the poor. He'd steal from the rich and keep it for himself."

"In an Oxo tin under the bed," George added.

Charlie laughed, more generously this time. "Hey, that's not bad. Do you mind if I pinch it?"

"Stand us a pint apiece and it's yours," Joe invited.

Charlie gave him a thumbs up. "Consider it done." With a final nod, he left them and wandered away towards the reception block.

Brenda scowled after him. "With a banana like him in charge of the entertainment, you can see what sort of a week we're in for. I hope he's not on stage when there are children in the audience."

Owen was more sanguine. "He doesn't sound as if he's especially blue."

Brenda cast a derisive eye on him. "You haven't seen his DVDs."

The inherent admission in her words surprised Joe. "You mean you have?"

Brenda sipped her tea and nodded. "It was when he was starting to fade on television. I'd seen him a time or two on the kind of variety programmes he was talking about. Good clean fun, all of it. But as his popularity went downhill, he started putting out these DVDs, and Colin bought one." At the mention of her late husband, her features clouded slightly. "Colin used to work for the Sanford colliery, remember, and he was no stranger to smutty jokes, but even he found it disgusting. Effing and jeffing every other word, racist, misogynist, even ageist." She scowled again. "Surely they'll have made him clean up his act for this place?"

"There'll be kids," George said. "Even at this time of year, people bring their sprogs to these places, so he won't get away with that kind of stuff, Brenda." He drank his tea. "Tell you what, though, he doesn't sound like a Cornishman."

Joe, too, had noticed the inflection in Charlie's voice. "West Midlands, I'd guess."

Brenda nodded. "He comes from somewhere on the outskirts of Birmingham if I remember rightly. He probably came down here when the television work dried up. A lot of the so-called comics start on the holiday camps, spend a few years in the spotlight, and then end up on the holiday camps again."

"Better than working for a living, I suppose." Joe spotted Les Tanner emerging from Reception and making his way towards them. "Hey up. It looks like we have lift-off."

***

Joe was surprised to find the bar quite full when he and Brenda entered shortly after 8 o'clock. He mentally remonstrated with himself. It should not be a surprise. During a recent visit to Cragshaven (to see Maddy Chester) he found resorts like Scarborough, Whitby, Bridlington still heaving with visitors enjoying the Indian summer. Here, the seventy members of the 3rd Age Club helped crowd the place, and as he scanned the room, he could see many of them preparing pens, highlighters and multi-coloured dabbers in preparation for the forthcoming bingo session.

They were scattered around tables on one side of the room, in their usual cliques, similar to those evident in the motorway cafeteria. Keith, their driver, sat apart among a small group of men who were probably fellow bus drivers.

Since checking in, he and Brenda had been busy, firstly unpacking, Brenda luxuriating in the comparative space allotted to the double room, Joe grumbling at the lack of same in the twin.

Joe microwaved them a simple meal of shepherd's pie, one of the frozen varieties which they had bought from the park shop. It was unsatisfactory, but after such a long journey, it was all either of them could be troubled with. They had a week in which to satisfy their more indulgent gastronomic fancies.

Brenda received a call on her tablet just after six, and both she and Joe were pleased to see Sheila's face appear on the screen. She had been in Boa Vista for a little over a week, and she had kept in touch with them back home in Sanford. She glowed with a healthy tan. The tropics obviously agreed with her.

The wi-fi connection was unreliable and the signal kept breaking up. Sheila blamed the second world technology of the Cape Verde Islands, but after their video call, Joe admitted to Brenda that the signals around Gittings were just as quirky. A couple of times he had phoned his nephew, Lee, to make sure he hadn't actually burned the café down, and he kept losing the signal, and when he tried to get online to evaluate the entertainment possibilities in the Hayle/St Ives, the free wi-fi, so heavily plugged in the brochure, broke the connection several times.

Sheila confirmed that she was enjoying her honeymoon, and praised Martin as a wonderful, attentive husband. Both Joe and Brenda kept their opinions to themselves. Joe felt too little time had elapsed since their wedding for Sheila to make a valid judgement, even though she had known the man for the better part of a year.

"A boyfriend and a husband are two different breeds," he later said to Brenda, "and I'll be interested to see what she has to say about him in a year's time."

They both wished Sheila their best, told her to enjoy her holiday, and looked forward to seeing her when they were reunited in Sanford, but there was a hint of sadness about both women that they were so far apart on different holidays.

"I do hope it works out for her," Brenda had said when the call was finally ended.

"She certainly deserves someone in her life. She's been on her own too long since Peter died." Joe eyed Brenda. "I think that goes for you, too."

Brenda would not hear it. "If you're thinking of proposing,

don't bother. I'm quite happy as I am, thank you. Gadding about where and with who I want."

"Whom," Joe corrected her.

"Womb?" She gave him a naughty wink. "Kindly leave my maternal bits and pieces out of this."

The worst moment came when they took turns to use the caravan's tiny bathroom. In order to allow Brenda a degree of privacy, Joe had secreted himself in the living room, leaving the pass door to the bedrooms closed. Not that either of them was particularly shy. When thinking of Weston-super-Mare earlier in the day, he recalled that at the time of that excursion, by mutual agreement he and Brenda were coming to the end of a brief, but enjoyable affair. That level of intimacy obviously meant that he had seen all of Brenda and vice versa. However, they were no longer involved, and simple respect meant that they were both entitled to their privacy.

Once in the entertainment centre, after collecting drinks for them – a Campari and soda for Brenda, and a half of bitter for himself – he joined her at a large table off to one side, where she sat with the Staineses, Les Tanner and Sylvia Goodson. With the various members' factions in mind, Joe reflected that there was nothing unusual about this group. Along with Sheila, the six of them were founding members of the 3rd Age Club and could regularly be found seated together on excursions or longer breaks.

He tucked himself into a seat alongside Brenda. "I'll tell you what, they don't half know how to charge in these places."

Alec Staines gulped down a sizeable mouthful of beer. "Almost as expensive as The Lazy Luncheonette."

Joe took the jibe in good part, and sipped at his beer. He grimaced convincingly. "Yes, but at least you're assured of quality when you come to my place."

Brenda vacated her seat, and made her way to the front of the room to queue up for bingo tickets, and Joe noticed that both Sylvia and Julia Staines were already prepared.

"Big money, is it?"

"I don't imagine so," Sylvia replied. "Just a few pounds."

"It's like playing the lottery, Joe," Julia told him. "A bit of fun with the prospect of winning some money."

"Boring is what I call it. When does the alleged entertainment start?"

"Half past nine," Les Tanner said. "No doubt they'll be anything but on time."

It was entirely in keeping with Tanner's attention to irrelevant detail, which in turn was part and parcel of his military training.

Unable to think of a suitable, scathing response, Joe glanced around the room again. "No sign of George and Owen."

Alec Staines, a self-employed painter and decorator, and a man with a level of calm equanimity almost perfectly at odds with Joe's cynicism, grunted. "You know what they're like. They've gone down into Hayle to see what the crack is."

Joe chuckled. "I've a suspicion that there's more life in St Ives, and the best they'll find in Hayle is a local folk band playing in a pub which used to be somebody's front room."

The unkind comment led to a brief debate on Cornish resorts, which Joe found uninteresting. He did not take many holidays, but when he did, he preferred Europe to the British Isles, and as far as he could recall, this was his first visit to Cornwall in over twenty years.

Brenda returned to the table, and the evening wore on, with several games of bingo, and to the congratulation of other members, Irene Pyecock won £15. After that, while two of the entertainment staff played party games with children in front of the stage, the remainder began to set up for what the brochure described as the 'Gittings All-Star Show'.

As Joe (and others) anticipated, it was a simple song and dance affair, concentrating on numbers from the musicals, with Wynette, the young woman Joe had seen arguing with Charlie Curnow earlier, taking the lead vocals, along with a lanky, shaggy haired individual whose name, as they eventually discovered, was Flick.

"I bet he gets called more than Flick," Joe said.

"Especially when people have had a few."

Taking into consideration their level of talent, the programme was quite good, but the tedium of the day was beginning to catch up on Joe, and by the time the show finished at quarter past ten, he was becoming restless, eager to get back to the van and catch up on his sleep.

At Brenda's insistence, he was at the bar queuing for the last drinks of the evening when Curnow came on stage, and while Joe waited, Wynette, the singer, made her way to the bar and stood next to him.

He gave her a pleasant smile and commented, "You don't like your boss's jokes?"

"Most of them are older than my mum," she replied in a rich, Cornish brogue. "He never got the hang of new comedy, didn't Charlie."

Joe would have agreed, but the barman, going by the unlikely name of Quint, arrived to serve him. As he pulled Joe's half of lager, he flicked a smile at Wynette. She responded with a face that could only be described as telling him where to go.

Ever intrigued by the interplay between people, Joe asked her, "Can I get you a drink?"

"No. I'm fine."

"Go on," Joe encouraged her. "At my age it's not like I'm expecting anything in return, is it?"

She smiled diffidently. "All right. Just a glass of cola, please." She hurried on to explain, "We're not allowed to drink when we're on duty."

Joe nodded to the barman. The lager was slow coming from the pump, and rather than stand there in thumb-twiddling silence, he engaged the young woman in conversation. "I couldn't help noticing the argument between you and Charlie, earlier today. Is he not giving you enough stage time?"

She chuckled. "Something like that. To be honest, I get fed up of working in places like this. When the park shuts at the end of the year, I do the pubs and clubs, and then back here for the beginning of the next season. But I'm better than that.

Ask anyone. I'm good enough to turn full-time professional."

Joe could not argue with her enthusiasm and motivation. Handing over the money for the drinks, he wished her, "The best of luck to you, too." He bid her a final good evening, and returned to his table, settling in for the remainder of Curnow's fifteen-minute spot.

From his point of view, Wynette had it wrong. Many of the comedian's quick-fire gags were as old as *his* mother, never mind hers, and ultimately, it wasn't just Joe glad to be on his way back to their holiday homes.

By half past eleven, having dispensed with a final cup of tea and a slice of toast to settle his stomach, he was in bed, and minutes later sound asleep.

Chapter Four

Joe was one of life's early risers. Even as a schoolboy, he had crawled out of bed early morning to help his father get the café ready for opening, and he had spent so many decades getting up in what many people would consider the middle of the night, that it was embedded into his system.

On Sunday morning, he slept a little longer than usual, but notwithstanding the tiring journey from Sanford, and the comparatively late night, he was still up before six.

Habit sent him to the bathroom first, where he washed and shaved. Running a café, albeit a truckers' haunt, demanded prominent levels of cleanliness, and shaving was a part of that hygiene. Like getting out of bed early, he had been carrying out the routine for so long, that it had become almost automatic.

Once dressed, he shuffled quietly about the caravan. Brenda was no stranger to early rising either. She and Sheila started work at seven every morning, and like him, they were usually up before six. Unlike him, Brenda was able to switch off when she was on holiday, and experience told him that she would not turn out until gone 8 o'clock. In deference to her, therefore, he kept the noise to a minimum.

Enjoying a bowl of cereal (which they had bought in the on-site supermarket at what Joe considered an extortionate price) and his first cup of tea of the day, he switched the television on, turned the volume down and activated the on-screen subtitles. National and local news didn't interest him in Sanford, and it was less appealing here in Cornwall, but he was interested in the weather forecast, and relieved to learn that although it would be chilly, especially at this early hour, the sun would shine for most of the day.

But that sun would not rise until after 7 o'clock. His light breakfast over, he stepped out of the caravan, and lit a cigarette. He was not surprised to find Alec Staines standing outside the van next door. Sylvia and Tanner were on the other side, and beyond them were George and Owen.

"Say what you like about Gittings," Alec said as he puffed on his own cigarette, "but they're well organised." He waved a hand at the nearby vans, the glowing tip of his cigarette describing wavy arcs in the night. "Most of the club are in this area."

"I shouldn't imagine it takes much organising at this time of year," Joe replied. Deliberately changing the subject, he asked, "How's business?"

"Busy. Making more than a butty. You know. Well you should know. You make a bloody fortune out of that café."

"So they say. But if I do, I also spend a fortune on trivia like rent, business rates, staff wages. The kind of outgoings you don't have." Joe glanced up at Alec's caravan. "Julia not seen the light of day yet?"

Alec snorted. "Chance'd be a fine thing. You'll be lucky to see her this side of nine o'clock. But Brenda's sleeping it off, as well."

"Got it in one, my son."

Alec drew on his cigarette again as Joe relit his.

"So what's the crack between you and Brenda, Joe? Only, we thought with Sheila getting spliced again—"

Joe cut him off. "Don't go there, Alec. Don't listen to any rumours. There's nothing between Brenda and me, and there's not likely to be. I see Maddy now and then, and you know what Brenda's like. If she doesn't hit on George Robson at least once this week, I'll drop my shorts on the town hall steps. And God help any other available man in this place."

Alec chuckled and crushed his cigarette underfoot. "Getting chilly. I'll catch you later."

He disappeared, leaving Joe alone, to stare up into the night sky. Somewhere over to the east, the first hint of dawn had appeared, dispelling all but the brighter stars in the

Western sky. It was a glorious sight, one they saw little of in Sanford, where street lighting blotted out the night. But for all that, Joe knew he could never consider living in this remote corner of England. He was a Sanfordian, and no matter how far he travelled, his heart would always drag him back to that former mining town.

An hour later, with the sun risen, he stepped out of the caravan again, but this time he was wearing a thick, quilted coat to combat the morning chill. Lighting his second cigarette of the day, he marched purposely to the west, and the low, grassy hill at the edge of the park. They had come four hundred miles, and so far he had seen no sign of the sea, other than occasional glimpses from the coach as it travelled through Avon, Somerset and Devon.

Others frowned upon his cigarette habit, and if he were truthful, it did affect his breathing, but as long as he was carrying an inhaler, he could cope with it, and despite the COPD, he kept himself fit – correction; his work kept him fit. Running a busy café might appear to be an easy life, especially for those who had never tried it, but Joe and his staff knew different. At peak times, such as early morning, when the truckers and the draymen of Sanford Brewery dropped in for breakfast, they were rushed off their feet, and that, combined with the heat of the kitchen, tended to sweat any excess weight off them, and the constant movement, zipping about the dining area, behind the counter, in and out of the kitchen, kept them active. Brenda might tend to excess weight occasionally, but Joe and Sheila were like rakes, and his nephew Lee, a huge man, had played rugby for the Sanford Bulls before a knee injury ended his career. Even so, he kept himself in the peak of physical condition with regular visits to a local gym.

Notwithstanding his chest problems, the march up the slight incline to the top of the grassy hill was no problem to him, and when he stood there, he bathed in the glorious sight.

Hayle beach was one of the broadest, longest, most spectacular in Great Britain. It spread before him, miles and miles of golden sand, glistening in the morning sunshine, and beyond it the sea lapped gently to the shore. Breathing in the wonderful sight, Joe consulted the geography maps in his head. The Bristol Channel? The Irish Sea? He had an idea that the Bristol Channel started much further up the coast, around North Devon, and the same, or similar, could be said of the Irish Sea. This, he recalled, was the Atlantic Ocean.

It was an awe-inspiring thought. If he jumped in a boat at the water's edge, and sailed west, he would land several thousand miles away in... New York? Florida? Somewhere like that (as it happened, Joe was wrong. Due west would land him in Newfoundland).

He found himself imagining the experience of sailors in the Middle Ages, staring out across such a vast and unchanging seascape, wondering if or when they would see land again. Easier these days, what with all the electronic navigation aids built into modern shipping, but back in the time of Columbus, Vespucci, Drake and Raleigh, they set sail effectively into the unknown.

What was it he had said to Brenda the previous day? He could do with more excitement in his life? He wondered idly whether he would have coped with the isolation, the thought of leaving the home country with no one for company but a crew of fellow, ragbag matelots.

And yet, he did not allow that thought to get to him. Instead he savoured the tang of ozone in the air, pushing fresh oxygen into his city-bound, smoke-damaged lungs. A light, onshore breeze rustled through the grass, tickled his cheeks and crept through his curly hair. If he had any doubts about the sanity of travelling so far for a holiday with the 3rd Age Club, this wonderful sight soon dispelled them. He was totally alone, and it was as if the entire world belonged to him, at least for the moment.

It did not last long.

The sound of a dog barking reached his ears, and brought his attention back to the beach, where he could see a woman, several hundred yards away, trying to drag her dog – a black Labrador – from a lump of... Joe did not know what... littering the sands. The sight annoyed him. Not the woman struggling with the mutt, but the fact that someone had dumped a van load of garbage on the beach, a fair lot of it by the looks of things. He was quite accustomed to fly tipping, but that was on the industrial landscape of Sanford, and especially prevalent amongst the tradesmen keen to get rid of the routine detritus of their days' work, but equally keen not to have to pay for its disposal. But here? On this wonderful, sparkling, clean beach? It was a disgrace.

A footpath, worn through the coarse grass by years of continuous use, led down to the sands. Taking his time, making sure he did not trip and fall, Joe made his way down until he was walking along the beach, his trainers sinking into it by half an inch or so, and leaving a trail of footprints behind him. He made for the water's edge, but before he reached it, he turned in the direction of the woman. She was two hundred yards from him, still struggling to pull the yapping dog away from what looked like a heap of discarded clothing. Joe's annoyance rose. Not fly tipping, then, but a couple who had obviously been doing what comes naturally, and didn't even bother to take their clothes with them when they were finished.

It seemed an unlikely scenario, although not impossible considering their proximity to a holiday park. Most such places had a reputation as knocking shops.

As he neared, he could see that he dog was not a black Labrador, but a Rottweiler, tugging and straining at the leash, barking so loud it could probably be heard in St Ives. It was obviously too strong for its mistress, a slender yet athletic forty-year-old wearing close fitting jeans and buried in a warm coat and woolly hat.

And as he got closer, he could hear her pointless pleas to the animal. "Come away, Bruiser. Come on. There's a good boy."

Bruiser was anything but a 'good boy'. He was clearly not listening. He pulled and tugged at his restraint, and every time she applied two hands to the strong, leather leash and pulled him away, he dragged her back.

Joe could not help smiling. It brought to mind a sketch he

had once seen in a sitcom, where a man was continually dragged off the set by an unseen dog. The performance of this woman on Bruiser was certainly better entertainment than the show he had watched the previous night, and much funnier than the sad, dated humour of Charlie Curnow.

"Could you use a little help?" Even as he called out, Joe's face was still spread with a large smile.

The woman registered his presence for the first time, and he could see that she was not only irritated with the dog, but in an advanced state of distress.

"Oh, thank God."

The dog became aware of Joe's proximity, and lost interest in the bundle of clothing, moving to stand between him and its mistress, its teeth bared, uttering a warning growl.

The woman scolded the dog once more. "Be quiet, Bruiser."

Joe had always been confident in the presence of dogs, and moving forward, he extended the back of his hand in a non-threatening gesture of friendship. While Bruiser checked him out, satisfying his natural instincts that this newcomer was not a threat, Joe concentrated on the woman.

His initial estimate of her age was about right, and from beneath her beanie, a fringe of dark hair showed above a brow creased with worry (or fear) and eyes that were streaming with tears.

"Whatever's the matter?"

She waved frantically at the clothing. "It's a young woman. I think she's… Oh, God, I can't believe it. I take the dog out for a walk and…"

She trailed off, and for the first time, Joe concentrated on the discarded clothing. His heart pounded, he began to circle, and as he reached the seaward side, he could see that it was, indeed, a young woman. Her legs and feet had been covered with a discarded coat, and the rest of her attire was hunched up around her shoulders, almost burying her. Her auburn hair was dishevelled, strewn around her face, which in turn was soaking wet, as if she had been here overnight, and affected by the tides (although Joe had no idea how far the incoming sea covered the broad sands). Her skin was pale and grey, her lips blue, and her brown eyes were open, staring emptily towards the ocean, one hand extended, as if she had perhaps tried to crawl away.

He had seen many deaths in his life, and was quite accustomed to seeing freshly deceased corpses. Normally, he would bend, press a finger to the neck in search of a pulse, but this time he did not bother. It was obvious that the girl was dead.

For a moment, he wondered who she was, and how she had come to die on this beach, but with a shock of recognition, he registered her identity. Winnie. The girl who had been arguing with Charlie Curnow the previous day while the 3rd Age Club waited for their caravans, the young woman who had been caterwauling into the microphone late last night, the same young woman he had spoken to at the bar.

That argument with Curnow suddenly assumed greater significance, but there was nothing about her body to suggest foul play, and given her occupation, and entertainments officer on a holiday park, there could be any number of reasons why she was on the beach. Drugs and drunkenness occurred to Joe right away.

Stepping away from the body, he took out his smartphone, but before dialling, he spoke to the woman who had discovered the body. "I'm Joe Murray. Down here on holiday. What's your name, luv?"

"Ava Garner."

Joe's hearing, quite accustomed to taking an order in the general cacophony of The Lazy Luncheonette, even when it came from the most quietly-spoken customer, was beset with the sound of the sea gently lapping the shore, and Bruiser's barking.

He clucked irritably. "You found a body on the beach, missus, and this is no time for taking the pi... mickey. Ava bloody Gardener."

Now she began to lose her temper. "Garner. G-A-R-N-E-R."

Joe apologised. "Can't you shut your dog up?"

She made a further effort to silence the animal, but with only minimal success, and Joe pressed on regardless.

"Right, Ava, we have to call the police, and you're gonna have to speak to them because you found the body, so you need to stay here with me. You're all right. You're perfectly safe with me, especially with your pet velociraptor at your side. But we can't leave until the police get here."

She nodded and made a determined effort to drag the dog further away, while Joe dialled 999.

After speaking with the police, and describing his location as precisely as he could, he rang Brenda, who answered with typical, Sunday morning annoyance.

"I wasn't planning on getting up for another hour, Joe. What the hell d'you want?"

As patiently as he could, he relayed the discovery, and concluded, "I'm likely to be back late."

Brenda sympathised, and promised to wait until he got back to the caravan before going out in search of their friends.

He cut the call and then walked away from the body, and stood with Ava.

Rolling a fresh cigarette, putting a light to it, he asked, "Are you local?"

She shook her head. "Oxfordshire. We're down here on holiday. Me, my husband, and two boys. You don't sound like a local, either."

Joe gazed sourly around the vast beach. Nothing had changed. The rising sun sparkled on the waters of the Atlantic, the sands spread away into the distance in both directions, and the light, autumn breeze, ruffled his hair and the coarse grass of the seashore. Yet it had lost the appeal of twenty minutes earlier.

"Yes," he repeated. "I'm down here with a bunch of friends, and we're from West Yorkshire." He took an irritable drag on his cigarette. "And right now, I wish I was back there."

Chapter Five

One of the first things Detective Sergeant Harriet O'Neill told them was that she liked to be addressed by her first name, and preferred it shortened to Hattie.

A few years younger than Ava, she had a pleasant, outgoing attitude, and her green eyes sparkled with enthusiasm. She too, was wrapped up in warm clothing, and from beneath the hem of her quilted coat, a pair of plain grey trousers could be seen, the cuffs settled around and above a pair of sensible, flat shoes.

While a couple of uniformed constables, the first people on the scene after Joe's call, set about cordoning off the area around the body and erecting the white shrouds that the forensic team needed, Hattie took statements from both Joe and Ava.

On the grassy rise above the beach, spectators had begun to arrive, simple black outlines, so distant that they gave the appearance of toy soldiers. But those soldiers were mobile. They shuffled along the path, occasionally turning their digital phones and cameras in the direction of events on the sand.

As well as being acclimatised to making statements to the police, Joe was equally used to the ghouls who hung around crime scenes with the inevitable interest in whatever was going on, and a barely subdued, macabre hope that they might catch sight of a body.

Joe had seen many such corpses, and aside from an investigative interest, they held no attraction. His assessment of this incident told that there would be nothing he needed to look into.

He kept his statement factual, and after confirming that he

and Ava were strangers, and had met on the beach less than an hour earlier, he could offer only one piece of information the police were not in possession of.

"I don't know the girl's name, other than it's Winnie. She's a singer at Gittings." He waved in the general direction of the holiday park above and behind them. "She was on stage last night, and that's how I know."

Ava confirmed it, Hattie thanked them, and invited them to go on their way. "Enjoy the rest of your holiday."

Bruiser pulled her along, and Ava made it back up the hill much faster than Joe who plodded along many yards behind her, and by the time he reached the brow, with the lines of vans spread out before him, she had disappeared.

He trudged down the slight incline to the caravan, and let himself in.

Brenda was seated at the small table, working her way through a bowl of muesli. As he came in, she stepped up to make some tea, but Joe told her to get on with the breakfast.

"I spend most of my life making tea, I'm sure I can rustle up a cup for myself." His stomach growled. "On the other hand, I'm starving. Ready for a decent breakfast, not a bowl of rabbit food." He cast a sour glance at her muesli.

"It's good for me, Joe. Good for you, too, if you bothered."

"Gar. You need a decent feed in you. I meanersay, how many truckers do we get in The Lazy Luncheonette asking for a bowl of hamster's bedding?"

Brenda refused to rise to his goading, he made himself a mug of tea, and joined her. While she carried on eating, he gave her a more detailed account of events on the beach, and she listened intently, asking the occasional and sometimes apparently pointless questions, such as whether Winnie was wearing her official Gittings' uniform.

It did not take long for Joe's irritation to show through. "What difference does it make what she was dressed in?"

"A lot of difference if it wasn't just a drunken accident. Suppose she was murdered?"

Joe gave the matter a moment's thought. "There was

nothing to say she had been killed, but even if she had, I still don't see what difference her clothing makes."

"You're the detective, Joe… or so you claim." Brenda swallowed the last mouthful of muesli, pushed the dish to one side and took a healthy slug of fresh orange juice. The taste sent shivers through her, and she put the glass down. "If she was wearing no clothes, it's a safe bet she didn't drown because it was too cold last night for skinny-dipping."

"She was fully clothed."

"Right. If she was still in her Gittings' uniform, it's odds-on that she was with someone from the staff. But if she was in her own clothes, then she could have been out with anyone, or even alone."

The light of realisation dawned in Joe's eyes. "I see where you're going now." He cast his mind back to the scene on the beach. "I don't think she was in her uniform. Course, murder would assume that she was actually with someone. She might have been on her own. In fact, if she was drunk or up to her eyes in drugs, she was more than likely alone. Anyone with her would have helped, wouldn't they?"

Brenda agreed but with reservations. "As long as they weren't drunk or up to their eyes in drugs too."

The circular argument was going nowhere, and Joe cleared the table and set about washing up the few dishes, while Brenda fussed around the van, tidying up.

Twenty minutes later, suitably attired in light, casual clothing, carrying warm coats over their arms against the possibility of the weather changing, they made their way to the entertainment centre, and the large cafeteria.

A quick glance around the dining area revealed that most of their fellow club members were already in residence. Brenda found a table close to Les Tanner and Sylvia Goodson, Alec and Julia Staines, and in the meantime, Joe queued up to order himself a full English breakfast and a cup of coffee for Brenda.

"Peckish?" Alec Staines asked as Joe joined them.

"Give me a dead rat and two stale loaves, and I'll show you how hungry I am."

Alec laughed. "I didn't ask what you serve at The Lazy Luncheonette."

"Bog off." Joe's final rejoinder was muttered through a mouthful of sausage and egg.

Inevitably, the moment Brenda told the table of Joe's encounter on the beach, the conversation turned to Winnie, the park in general, and via a circuitous route concentrated once more on Joe.

"That will make your holiday, won't it, Murray?" Les Tanner said with a cynical smirk.

Joe, in the act of finishing his meal, shook his head. "Nothing suspicious about it, Les, so I refuse to get involved. I'm down here for a holiday."

Sylvia and Julia murmured their agreement.

"It's about time you had a proper rest," Sylvia observed.

Julia Staines was more mocking. "It's also about time you opened your wallet and gave it some fresh air as well as exercising those poor fivers."

Her husband laughed out loud. "Fivers? You mean fifties."

Quite at home with this kind of repartee, Joe replied, "I don't have to come here for this kind of abuse, you know."

Brenda was quicker off the mark than the others. "That's right. He can go anywhere."

Across the cafeteria, George Robson sauntered in and sent Owen Frickley to the counter. It was a reflection on their long-time friendship. George was clearly the leader of the pair, and Owen the follower.

George appeared badly hungover, which again was no surprise. Joe's age, overweight and divorced, he lived purely for enjoyment, a large part of which consisted of heavy drinking. He scanned the room, and his eyes lighted on Joe. He weaved his way through the tables and stood alongside them.

"Hey up, Joe. There's a biddy out there looking for you." He waved an arm towards the exit.

"Who?"

"Middle-aged bint. Dressed in the same uniform as the rest of the crew here. Got a face like Huddersfield."

Joe feigned puzzlement. "And what does someone who comes from Huddersfield look like?"

"I didn't say she looks like she's *from* Huddersfield. I said she looks *like* Huddersfield. You know. Clapped-out and past her sell by date."

"Well, she can wait until I've finished my breakfast. What were you and Owen up to last night?"

George took the seat next to Joe. "Out for a few bevvies in Hayle. Talk about boring. It should be called Hell not Hayle. We ended up at this pub with a local folk band and people dancing. One of the local yokels reckoned it was a kayleigh, but, I'll tell you what, they don't know how to spell down here. The way I read the sign, it said 'say-e-lid', with an H on the end."

Joe shook his head sadly, Brenda tittered. "In Gaelic, the word is spelled C-E-I-L-I-D-H. You're just showing your ignorance, George."

"No I'm not. It just goes to prove what I said. How could anyone spell ceilidh like that? It doesn't make sense."

Joe finished his meal, drained off his teacup, got to his feet. "Stick to Yorkshire, George. I'd better see what this woman wants. I don't suppose she has a name?"

"It might be drop dead," George replied with a broad grin. "That's what she said when I asked her if she fancied a couple of pints tonight."

With a sombre thought that not much changed in the world of the Sanford 3rd Age Club, Joe left the cafeteria, and strolled out into the open spread of the gaming area, where the whistles, beeps, and bells of slot machines, electronic games, and the like, filled the air, entertaining children and teenagers. It caused him to wonder why they were not at school, but he had never been blessed with parenthood, and the mysteries of bringing up and keeping children occupied, remained just that; a mystery.

There were a couple of security guards standing by the door, listening to a woman in company uniform, and Joe assumed that this was the person who had been seeking him. He crossed the thickly carpeted floor, and stood a respectful distance from her, but within the arc of her peripheral vision.

He estimated her age at about fifty years. Slightly taller than him, she obviously took care of herself, maintaining a slim figure. Her suntan was not excessive, but her eyes were creased with what could be years of sun-worshipping, laughter or worry. She wore no make-up, but her light brown hair appeared professionally set and cared for, and he could imagine her taking an hour off to visit the hairdresser weekly or perhaps monthly. A glance at her slender hands, revealed no rings, but finely manicured nails and a hint of delicacy about the skin.

Finished with the security guards, she turned to face him, and he took in her nametag: *Eleanor Dorning, General Manager*.

She gave him a pleasant smile. "Can I help you, sir?"

"Well, you could start by not calling me sir. I'm not an officer, and most people say I'm not a gentleman, either." Joe smiled to show he was joking. "My name's Joe Murray. Apparently, a member of your staff has been looking for me."

"Ah. Yes, Mr Murray, that would be me, but it's the police who want to speak to you. About Wynette Kalinowski." Her face fell a little at the mention of the dead woman's name.

"Right. Point me to them."

"The inspector's taken a small office in the reception. I'll walk over there with you."

They left the building, stepping out into the balmy, autumn sunshine. The rising temperature had already evaporated the sparkling dew, and carried with it the promise of another warm, dry, September day. From the flowerbeds, the scent of roses and lavender reached Joe's nostrils, and mingled with Eleanor's perfume, not expensive, and not overpowering. Even though he was faced with a police interview, the waves of relaxation washed over him.

He assumed that the forthcoming meeting would be no more than a formal statement with an unknown in the shape of the local CID. Once again, he assumed it was CID, but it was uncertain because O'Neill had insisted she was a sergeant, while Eleanor said the officer he was about to see was an inspector. Not that it made a great deal of difference to Joe. He was used to dealing with police officers from local, community constables, all the way up to the Assistant Chief Constable. He had dealt with the friendly, the unfriendly, the contingent, the bullying, those who were willing to accept his assistance, those who were not, and to a man (or woman) they could not intimidate him.

He became conscious of the silence between himself and the woman alongside him. "Cornwall born and bred, were you, Mrs Dorning? Only you don't sound it."

"It's Ms Dorning, but please call me Eleanor. And yes, I am, Mr Murray."

"I'll call you Eleanor if you promise to call me Joe."

"Deal." Her accent was a cultured, classless English, without any trace of the local drawl. "I come from Truro. It's about twenty miles from here, a little over half way between here and Newquay. University and teacher training knocked the Cornish burr out of me." She chuckled.

Joe wondered why she gave up teaching, and why anyone with a university education would want to manage a caravan park, then decided it was none of his business. Aside from tourism, he imagined that work would be difficult to come by in this area.

He confined himself to neutral, complimentary comments. "You have a beautiful part of the country. One of the best beaches I've ever seen."

Eleanor smiled indulgently. "Thank you. I imagine your part of the world isn't as smoky and grimy as we all imagine."

Joe could not help laughing. "That impression belongs back in the fifties, or even before the war. I come from a little place called Sanford, about twenty miles from Leeds. It was a mining town, and we had a huge foundry, and between them they employed most of the men folk in town. But they're both long gone. They've given way to new, more modern industries."

"No whippets and flat caps?"

He laughed again. "I have a flat cap, but I don't have a

whippet, and I don't know anyone who does."

They were nearing the reception entrance. "So what do you do, Joe?"

"Like you, I'm in catering. Only I run a workmen's café. Mainly truckers, you know, but we're on the ground floor of a brand-new development, full of offices, so we get to feed the clerks and telesales people too."

"Profitable, I imagine. People will always need feeding."

Joe became more guarded. "I don't make as much as people think, but it gives me an above-average lifestyle." He grinned. "Enough to bring me to Cornwall in late September."

They paused outside the entrance to Reception. "I'll have a cup of tea ready for when the police have done giving you the third degree."

"Don't worry about me, lass. I've dealt with more than my fair share of coppers." Joe took in her look of surprise and hastened to explain. "I do some part-time work for insurance companies as a private investigator, and as well as that, my niece and her boyfriend are both detectives in West Yorkshire."

Eleanor appeared reassured, and Joe went on.

"Besides, how much can I tell him? It's a simple drowning, isn't it?"

Eleanor's hand flew to her mouth. "Oh my God. You don't know do you?"

All Joe's senses came to full alert. "What don't I know?"

"Winnie didn't drown. She was strangled." Her eyes burned into him. "It's not an accident. It's murder."

Chapter Six

Detective Inspector Richard Howell was probably somewhere in his mid-40s. Tall, languorous, but with broad shoulders and large hands, he was dressed in a pair of light grey trousers and a navy blue blazer, with a blue shirt highlighting a dark blue tie bearing the badge of either the police service or a military regiment. He enjoyed a head of neatly combed almost black hair, beneath which was a clear brow and a pair of diamond blue eyes, which were, unfortunately, narrowed into an accusing stare, matching the grim set of his thin lips.

"You're Murray?"

The uninviting snap of Howell's gravelly voice, ignited Joe's irritation. "No. I'm Joe Murray."

The loathing in the inspector's eyes seemed to increase. "That's what I said."

"No. You said Murray. Where I come from, even the filth have the courtesy to treat people with... er... courtesy. They'd ask if I was Joe Murray or Mr Murray, not treat me like a schoolboy up before the headmaster."

Howell waved at the seat on the other side of the desk. "Just sit down." Joe took the chair and waited patiently while the inspector checked his thin notes. "You found the body."

It was not a question, but Joe interpreted it as one. "No. That was a woman walking her dog on the beach... Well, actually it was the dog that found the body."

Howell poised his pen. "Name?"

It seemed to Joe to be an odd question, and he frowned. "Bruiser, if I recall."

Howell made a note. "First name?"

Joe's mystification increased. "I didn't know that dogs had first names."

Howell's face disfigured into a mask of blind fury. "Not

the bloody dog. The woman."

Joe met the virulent anger with some of his own. "Then why don't you learn to speak English. I said the dog found the body, and you asked me its name." He leaned forward and jabbed his finger into the desktop. "Her name was Ava Garner."

The announcement did nothing to appease Howell. "Listen to me, Murray, I'm already having one of those days, and I'm in no mood for you taking the—"

Joe cut him off. "I thought the same thing, but apparently her name really is Ava Garner. She's staying somewhere on this park. You need to speak to Eleanor Dorning, the general manager." He took a couple of deep, calming breaths. "Your sergeant should have told you all this."

"I haven't seen O'Neill yet. I only spoke to her on the phone. She's still busy on the beach, sorting out forensics and arranging for the body to be shifted. She gave me your name and nothing else."

"That's because Mrs Garner was in a bit of a state. Well, she would be, wouldn't she? It's not every day you take the dog for a walk and find a body on the beach."

His head lowered, eyes fixed on his notebook where he was scribbling down the information, Howell ignored the remark. "Address?"

Joe shrugged. "Search me. Somewhere in Oxfordshire, she said."

"Not Ava bleeding Garner. Your address."

"Are conversations with you always this confusing?" Joe asked, and received a glower of thunder by return.

"What is your address?"

"The Lazy Luncheonette, Doncaster Road, Sanford, West Yorkshire."

Suspecting another attempt to confuse the issue, Howell demanded, "That some kind of diner, is it? And you live there, do you?"

Joe, too, was beginning to tire of the convoluted exchange. "It's a truck stop, *my* truck stop. I own the place, and I live above it."

It was not true. He had lived above the old Lazy Luncheonette, but that building had burned down before the new one was put up. However, he was rarely to be found in his council flat on Leeds Road, and the easiest way for the police to contact him, should they need to, was at The Lazy Luncheonette.

"Right. So what were you and this Garner woman doing on the beach this morning?"

"She was struggling with her dog, and I was going for a walk."

"How long have you known her?"

"I don't know her. I met her this morning."

"And you both happened to stumble across the body?" Disbelief marinated in suspicion poured through the inspector's words.

"What is this? Are you accusing me of something, Howell? I thought I was coming here to give a simple statement after finding the dead woman, and I don't expect to be accused of murdering her."

Still busy making notes, Howell looked up sharply. "Who said she was murdered?"

"The same Eleanor Dorning who'll put you onto Ava Garner and Bruiser when you get round to asking her. And while I think on, that dog doesn't like people; especially when they come full of attitude."

Howell's phone rang. He studied the menu window, and irritably cut it off. Using his pen as a pointer, he bit back at Joe. "The only one here with an attitude is you. You say you were just out for a walk?"

"Yes. It's the kind of thing we do a lot in Yorkshire. We have to. Our whippets need exercising."

The inspector half rose, ready to fight back against the cynical response, but Joe pressed on.

"I went for a walk. There's nothing odd about that. I'm on holiday. I wanted to see the sea because you can't see it from our caravan, and I can't see it from home, either, because it's sixty miles away."

Howell was about to interrupt, but Joe's flow was

unstoppable.

"When I got to the beach, Mrs Garner was struggling with the dog, and I went to see if I could help. She pointed out that the bundle of rags I'd seen on the sand was actually a dead woman. From there, I called the police, and stood by with Mrs Garner to ensure that no one else could disturb your crime scene. When your sergeant turned up, I told her who the girl was, and she told Mrs Garner and me to get the hell outta there while your forensic people got to work. That's it, Howell. That's your lot. That's all I know."

The inspector resumed his seat while Joe was ranting at him, and when he spoke, the suspicion was still evident. "And how did you know who the dead woman was. She's a local girl, yet you claim to be from four hundred miles away. So how did you know?"

"Because I was talking to her in the bar last night. She was the star turn of the evening. And I didn't know who she was. I just knew her name and what she did. You obviously think I have something to do with her death, Howell, so let me ask you this; how did she die?"

"We haven't had the medical examiner's report yet."

"Eleanor Dorning told me that Winnie was strangled." Joe held up his hands. "Notice how small my hands are. Compare them to any marks you may find on her. And if you want my fingerprints, you're welcome to them, but you don't have to take them. Get in touch with the Sanford police. They already have them. The same goes for my DNA fingerprint."

If anything Joe's final words seemed to firm up Howell's suspicions. A look of disgusted satisfaction crossed his face. "I knew there was something about you. How many times have you been hauled in by the Sanford plod?"

"Twice," Joe admitted. "Both times they accused me of murder, and both times I proved them wrong. If you wanna waste money on a phone call, speak to Chief Superintendent Don Oughton. He's the station commander there, and an old friend. He'll vouch for me. Now are you done with me, or do you want to accuse me of something else? Like nicking the bulb out of the Eddystone Lighthouse?"

"You can go for now. But don't wander far, I might need to speak to you again."

Joe got to his feet, took a couple of paces to the door, stopped, turned and came back. "There is one other thing."

Howell let out a heavy sigh. "What now?"

"When we got here yesterday afternoon, we had to wait before our accommodation was ready. Three friends and I were having a cup of coffee outside the cafeteria, and the dead woman came wandering in with Charlie Curnow, the park comedian. They were arguing the toss over something. All I could hear was Charlie warning her to shut up and get on with her job, and she warned him that she knew something about him."

Howell made hurried notes. "I'll look into it, but it's probably nothing. We know Charlie Curnow well, but bumping off some little tart like this isn't his form."

"That's what they said about the woman who tried to kill me in Majorca."

Without waiting for further questions, Joe marched out of the room.

When he emerged into the reception area, he found Eleanor Dorning seated in a comfortable armchair by the window, waiting for him with the promised cup of tea, and he joined her, taking the chair opposite, staring angrily out across the open area of the camp entrance. Cars were coming and going, people were making their way to and from the entertainment centre, and outside the cafeteria, he could see some of his friends enjoying a mid-morning cup of coffee. It was the usual clique of Brenda, George and Owen, Alec and Julia, Tanner and Sylvia, but now joined by Stewart Dalmer, a former College tutor and part-time antiques dealer. Joe guessed, but was not certain, that after Whitby, where Brenda and Dalmer had been teamed up for the treasure hunt, some kind of fleeting relationship had developed between them. Brenda, certainly, had an unjustified reputation for being free and easy with her favours, but Joe knew different. She dated a number of men, but she was not leaping into bed with any of them.

Eleanor poured tea for them, passed the cup and saucer across to Joe, and settled back into the seat, her face exhibiting concern for him. "Inspector Howell is in one of his usual strops, isn't he?"

Joe nodded. "You know him?"

She nodded as she sipped her tea. "He has a downer on Gittings. It's as simple as that. This is a small town, Joe, and we don't get a lot of trouble, but if you listen to Howell, the vast majority of his time is taken up dealing with drunkenness on this park."

"And is it?"

"No. We get the occasional incident, true. Perhaps once, maybe twice in a season, and our security people are quick to jump on it, but obviously, they only have certain powers, and when it gets too bad, we have to call the police. Most times, it's Sergeant O'Neill, but Howell's had to deal with issues now and again. He's just one of life's grumblers. I think he fancies himself as a hotshot detective, who should be working in London, rather than a country copper with a large beat which spreads from here to Helston, down to Penzance, back here via Land's End and St Ives."

Joe disregarded much of the geography lesson. "But this is the first time he's had to investigate a murder on your premises?"

"To my knowledge, yes. It's a shocking business, Joe, and it won't do our image any good. I informed the regional director's office first thing this morning, and no doubt, I can expect a visit from him later in the week."

"Nasty?"

"Well, certainly unpleasant. Believe it or not, this is a very competitive industry, which is why Gittings almost went under. They were taken over by a national company about five years ago. The company has half a dozen parks in the Devon and Cornwall area, and the regional director has enough on his plate trying to keep on top of one problem or another, without Gittings going into virtual lockdown because one of the staff has been murdered."

Joe was beginning to relax in the woman's company, but

he felt it necessary to challenge her words. "Surprise, surprise I'm not concerned with the attitude of your big boss. My concern is the death of this young woman. I mean, how old was she? Twenty-five, thirty?"

"Twenty-seven," Eleanor replied, and smiled at Joe's raised eyebrows. "The moment I heard, I had to dig out her personnel file."

"That explains how you could be so certain about her age. Tell me something, Eleanor, what was her relationship with Charlie Curnow?"

"He was her immediate boss. Charlie is our entertainments manager. All the entertainment staff are answerable immediately to him. Why do you ask?"

As he drank more tea, Joe told her of the incident he had witnessed the day before, the threat Charlie had thrown at Winnie, and her response.

"I know a lot about murder," he concluded. "I've investigated my fair share of them, and I was actually the target of one killer."

Eleanor gasped. "Really?"

"Really. When you boil it all down, there are only two serious motives for deliberately taking someone's life; sex and money. I don't know what went on between the pair yesterday, but they were arguing as they came from the car park, but Winnie's final remark sounded to me like blackmail. In other words, he daren't sack her because if he did, she'd open up about what she knew. And what kind of information is it that blackmailers usually hold over their victims? Sex or money. Assuming the killer wasn't a plain psycho, it's usually one or the other behind every incident of this nature. What do you know about Charlie? What could he be up to that might get him into trouble? What do you know that might make it worth his while to murder the girl?"

"Nothing."

Eleanor looked around the room to ensure that no one was paying any attention. She need not have worried. The few clerks on duty were all busy with one or another of the routine tasks their work entailed, and no one even registered their presence.

Nevertheless, she leaned across the table and lowered her voice. "Between the two of us, I don't care for Charlie. And it's not because of his low comedy. I don't like the man personally. He's a drunk. You can smell it on him even at lunchtime, before he's had the chance to get any more inside him. Trouble is, Joe, as you're probably aware, you can't choose the people you work with, and despite his personal shortcomings and rubbish jokes, he's good at his job. Aside from the people who own caravans on this site, the park is closed between New Year and mid-March, and during that time, Charlie auditions new applicants, and whips them into shape for the new season. He works them like sleigh dogs in the Arctic, and by the time we come to open up again in the middle of March, they're at their best. And it doesn't stop there. He drives them through rehearsals throughout the season. He never lets up, and when he gets someone who's not up to scratch, he doesn't hesitate. He fires them."

Joe took in the information, and slotted it into the filing cabinets of his mind, creating a new folder and naming it, *Wynette Kalinowski*.

"One of my friends was telling me that she bought a DVD of Charlie's act, and it was, er, let's say, *adult*. Am I right in assuming he doesn't put that kind of act on here?"

"I wouldn't have it, Joe. We have children on site all year round. There is no way I would tolerate Charlie putting on that kind of act."

"And suppose he was putting on private shows, away from the main entertainment complex? He could be making a bob or two on the side."

Eleanor shook her head and finished her tea. "He'd also be taking a hell of a chance with his job. He's not the only one who's hard with his staff. If I found him doing anything of the sort, I'd fire him like that." She clicked her fingers to emphasise the point.

Joe smiled, finished his tea, slid the cup and saucer back across the table to her and got to his feet. "Thanks, Eleanor. You've given me food for thought."

Chapter Seven

The 3rd Agers of Sanford had two or three excursions planned for during the week, but it was Sunday, which had always been scheduled as a rest day (to get over the long journey) and there was nothing on their itinerary other than hanging around Gittings Holiday Park or making their way down into Hayle.

After giving his friends an account of the brusque meeting with Howell, Joe suggested they walk into the town, in search of lunch.

"You'll be piling the pounds on if you're not careful, Joe," Brenda said.

"And you'll be lucky if they understand the idea of lunch," George Robson commented.

Joe ignored the ribaldry and a little after half past twelve, while George and Owen went in search of a lunchtime drink, the rest of the group, the Staineses, Tanner and Sylvia, Brenda and Dalmer, left the park via the coastal path, and made their way towards the town.

The estuary upon which Hayle sat was the confluence of a number of rivers, but in Joe's humble opinion, describing them as rivers was an exaggeration. The recent warm spell saw them shallow, the sandbanks exposed, and little in the way of boats on the narrow channels.

With his customary candour, his grumpiness enhanced by the ill-tempered confrontation with the police inspector, Joe declared the town 'boring' and lacking the amenities usually found in a seaside haunt.

"I think most people make for St Ives," Sylvia said. "It's only a few miles around the headland."

Nevertheless they found a pub which served an adequate

Sunday roast, after which they took a tour of the main street, and the few shops that were open. By four o'clock, they were on their way back to Gittings, but having walked down, they chose to take taxis to avoid climbing the hills.

Throughout the afternoon and the return journey, they ran through a series of variable conversations, discussing everything and anything from Cornwall to Yorkshire, the boost or otherwise that Brexit might bring to the Cornish Peninsula and the British seaside in general, and a host of other trivial, inconsequential subjects. Joe had only half a mind on their chatter. He was more concerned with the death of Wynette Kalinowski, his mind's eye constantly replaying the argument he had seen between her and Charlie Curnow the previous day.

He knew that Howell would be unhelpful, to say the least, but he also knew that the man would contact Don Oughton in Sanford, which might prompt Hattie O'Neill to open up a little more than her boss.

Joe's experience of crime in general, murder in particular, told him not to prejudge anything. He knew so little about the victim. She had something on Charlie Curnow, but it did not follow that Curnow had murdered her. In Joe's opinion, the best witness to any crime was the victim, and he would need to learn an awful lot more about her before he could point an accusing finger at anyone.

Curnow was a good start point, and when they got back to Gittings, while Brenda made her way to the bedroom for an afternoon nap, Joe went in search of the camp clown.

He asked at Reception, was told he would find Curnow behind the scenes in the show bar, and when Joe wandered behind the backstage curtain, he found the area a hive of activity.

The crew, most of whom he had seen on stage the previous night dancing or accompanying Winnie in her songs, were busy shifting basic scenery into place, presumably for the evening's show. Another was touching up a jungle-style backdrop from a can of paint, and to one side, a technician (Joe assumed he was such because he did not recognise the man from the previous night) was changing a bulb in one of the lighting gantries.

Clad in the same shabby, fawn trousers and trainers he wore when they first met, Curnow was sat at a makeshift desk off to one side, a small, tatty, dark green rucksack between his feet, and a half empty whiskey glass at his elbow. His brow creased as he looked over a morass of papers which looked like scripts.

Joe ambled across to him and the park comic looked up and scowled. "I'm busy. What do you want?"

"A word."

"I should have thought you'd had enough words for one day. That copper gave me a right going over after what you said to him."

"I told him what I saw, Charlie. I didn't accuse you of anything."

"Just as well, cos I didn't do anything. Now, like I said, I'm busy trying to rearrange things without her." He gestured at the sea of paperwork before him. "Clear off."

Joe ignored him, looked around, found a chair, dragged it to the dressing table on which Curnow was working, and sat down. The comic's temper, clearly on display when he dealt with Winnie on the car park, was visibly rising.

"I don't only run a café, you know. I'm a private investigator, too. I do odds and sods of investigative work for a local insurance company."

"I suppose you need them up there. All you Yorkies are known fiddlers, aren't you?"

Joe chuckled. "Insulting my ancestry won't work. You're a Brummie, and they know how to fiddle their tax receipts the same as anyone." He leaned on the table and it rocked precariously, swilling whiskey around Curnow's glass. "Thing is, I've investigated my fair share of murders in my time, and is not much that escapes me. If you're in the frame, it's because Howell had to get out of bed early on a Sunday morning, and not because I dropped you in it. All I said was I saw you arguing with her yesterday, and I heard her threaten you. What is it she knew about you, Charlie?"

He glared at Joe. "Read my lips. Sod… off."

Joe shrugged easily. "Suit yourself. Your local filth will be all over this place like a cheap suit, and I know the cops. They'll nick anyone they think they can charge, whether they're guilty or not. I'm different. I look for evidence, I look for things the police miss, and when I find them – and you can be sure I will – then I accuse. From my point of view, Winnie threatened you, and she looked dangerous enough to hint that whatever she knew, it could cause you a lot of grief." Joe stood up. "Trust me, I will find out, and if I twigged that it might just be enough for you to shuffle her off the mortal coil, I'll take it to plod." He marched away.

"Just a minute, Murray."

A satisfied smile crossed Joe's lips before he turned. "Yes?"

Curnow pointed to the empty chair where Joe had been sitting, and Joe walked back and took a seat again.

"You're not the only one who notices things," Curnow said. "When I bumped into you outside the café yesterday, I noticed you roll your own. How much do you pay for your tobacco?"

"What's this got to do with what we're talking about, Charlie?"

"A lot. Just answer the question."

Joe racked his brain. "It depends where I buy it. It's cheaper from the wholesaler when I go for supplies for the café, but it gets involved tax-wise, and obviously they only sell it by the carton. If I buy from a newsagent or tobacconist, it costs me about eleven notes for a single pack."

Charlie lifted the rucksack. It reminded Joe of his own. Olive green, with four side pockets, two of them zip-up, the flap fastened with plastic spring clips, the webbing straps with comfort pads for the shoulders. Curnow sprung open the top flap and dug into it, before coming out with a pack of hand-rolling tobacco.

He offered it. "Six quid to you, no questions asked."

Joe took the pack from him, and turned it over in his hand. It was sealed in transparent plastic, just the same as the packs he always bought, but on those he purchased from the wholesalers or newsagents, there was a distinctive label which declared it to be 'UK – duty paid'. This pack lacked any such label.

"Contraband?"

"I told you. No questions asked. You want it?"

Joe had no hesitation. He dug into his pockets, came out with a handful of change, counted out £6 and handed it over. "Now—"

Curnow cut him off. "That's what Winnie Kalinowski thought she knew about me. The wages here are crap, my ex-wife is expensive, and I have to top my funds up. And I'll tell you something else, she could go to whoever she wanted with the information. I don't care. If the filth nick me, the worst they'll do is take whatever stocks I have. I can have a fresh load in within ten minutes of coming out of court. Now do you understand?"

Joe tucked the tobacco into his pocket and got to his feet. "Why didn't you say so?"

As he walked away, Curnow's voice stopped him again.

"I can tell you this, Murray."

Joe turned and faced the comedian, and was confronted by a smile of joyous malevolence.

"Winnie was a spiteful, vicious little cow, and I wasn't the only one she tried to get her claws into."

***

The afternoon sun was dipping towards the Western horizon and the temperature had begun to cool when Joe emerged from the entertainment complex. A quick glance at his watch revealed that it was almost half past five, and he had been talking with Curnow for the better end of forty-five minutes.

As he made his way past Reception, Eleanor Dorning, Howell and Hattie came out of the building. Eleanor laid a generous smile on him, Hattie too, but the inspector was exactly the opposite, and made a beeline for Joe.

"I have news for you, pal. You're not outta the woods."

Joe rose to the challenge. "Have you ever considered another career, Howell? Maybe a customer service advisor for the Houses of Parliament? What the hell are you talking about?"

"Turns out Winnie the stiff wasn't strangled. She was knifed. Under the rib cage. Hours before the Garner woman and her mutt found her. So don't waffle to me about the size of your hands, Murray. Anyone can jam a knife into a body."

"Yeah, and anyone could jam a knife into your head, open it up and search for a brain. Do you have any evidence to link me to this girl's death?"

"We're looking for it."

"Well, until you find it, get off my case."

Joe marched away and barely heard Howell instruct Hattie to follow, and speak to him. He was at the caravan, unlocking the door when she caught him up.

"I'm sorry, Mr Murray, but the boss has insisting I talk to you."

"As long as your attitude is better than his, it's no problem. Come in. I'll make us a cup of tea."

There was no sign of Brenda, but the far bedroom door was closed, and Joe assumed she was still taking her afternoon nap. Putting a finger to his lips, he said, "We'll have to keep the noise down. Brenda's asleep in the back room."

Hattie nodded, removed her topcoat and sat down at the table while Joe switched on the kettle, and took down cups from the overhead cupboard. Preparing the brews and waiting for the kettle to boil, he asked, "What is it with Howell?"

Hattie sighed. "He's like that most of the time, especially when we have to deal with these caravan parks. We get a lot of trouble on them."

"Not according to Eleanor Dorning. She admitted that there is some bother, but it's minimal; no more than two or three incidents a year."

The kettle snapped off, and Joe busied himself preparing cups of tea. He put the sugar basin on the table for Hattie to help herself, and poured a little milk into a small, stainless steel jug, which he then carried to the table.

Hattie declined the sugar, clicked a couple of artificial sweeteners into her cup, and stirred vigorously.

As she did so, she replied to Joe's observation. "Eleanor's being a bit… What's the word… not exactly dishonest, but…" She trailed off, groping for the correct word.

"Devious?" Joe suggested as he joined her.

"Not quite. She's minimising the problem." She sipped the tea with approval. "God, I needed that. I've been on that rotten beach most of the day, and frankly, I've had enough for one Sunday."

"My niece is a detective inspector in Sanford, so I know where you're coming from."

"Yes, I know. Howell insisted I ring them, and speak to the chief superintendent there, but he wasn't in, so I ended up speaking to DI Gemma Craddock, and she told me she was your niece. She also told me that if we didn't keep you in check, you'll solve this killing before we get anywhere near."

Hattie giggled, and Joe had to divert his eyes from her ample breasts, which wobbled suggestively as she laughed. He always told himself that his hit and miss relationship with Maddy Chester was sufficient to keep his libido in check, but there were times when…

He brought his rambling thoughts under control. "Gemma's being a bit too kind there. It's true, I do poke my nose in where it doesn't concern me, and I usually get it right, but that's not to say that the police are a total load of numpties. It all depends on the SIO. Some are happy to accept my help, others aren't. Your boss falls into the latter category, and before we go any further, I can tell you that this is not the first time I've been suspected of actually committing the murder."

"I know that, too. Gemma told me. Ritchie – Inspector Howell – is a bit of a control freak, and he's not happy with the idea of someone like you poking around, and it makes it worse that it's on Gittings."

"Which brings us back to Eleanor Dorning and her

insistence that there's no trouble here."

Hattie drank more tea, and Joe left his seat, dipped into the overhead cupboard again and came out with two packets of biscuits, which he placed on the table. He took a digestive, and invited Hattie to help herself.

"So what's the real situation with Gittings?"

Hattie, chewing through a rich tea biscuit, waited a moment until she had swallowed a mouthful, and then said, "It's not just here. There are half a dozen caravan parks in this area, and they all have the same problem. Theft."

Joe was unimpressed. "I should imagine it's a fairly common problem in seaside resorts anywhere. People on holiday tend to be less careful about their possessions. Plus, you have any number of strangers coming into your accommodation; cleaners and the like."

"Bang on the mark," Hattie replied. "Without exception, these parks use contract cleaners, and no matter which park we're talking about, they all work for the same company, based in Penzance, but employing local people for their various contracts: here, Newquay, Bude, Mousehole, Falmouth, wherever. They usually have the contract for cleaning whichever caravan park or holiday camp is concerned, but the thieving seems to be concentrated in this area; Hayle and St Ives. And the stuff which is taken is the usual. Money, if it's left lying around, and small items which can be sold fairly quickly."

"Cameras, phones, that kind of thing?"

"Yep. There's any number of second-hand dealers all over the county who're happy to buy that kind of stuff." Hattie helped herself to a second biscuit. "You don't mind, do you? I didn't get much lunch."

"Help yourself."

Joe ruminated for a moment while Hattie finished her second biscuit. "And this is what Howell wanted you to tell me when he asked you to have a word?"

"No." Hattie paused a moment as if wondering how to put the truth to Joe. "It wasn't immediately obvious that Winnie he had been stabbed. The doc found out when he removed the clothing she was buried under, and he told me right away. I tried to ring Ritchie, but he didn't answer. I get the feeling he was with you at the time."

Joe agreed. "I remember his phone ringing while we were talking, and he cut the call off."

"The thing is, Mr Murray, you can't be cleared of suspicion. Mrs Garner found the body, and she's in the frame, too. I'm not saying he seriously suspects either of you, but unless and until you can satisfactorily account for your movements between, say midnight and three o'clock this morning, you stay on our list."

"I don't think that's a problem. I was here all night, sleeping the journey off, and no, there are no witnesses to that."

Hattie cast a glance towards the closed door leading to the bedrooms. "Your wife can't—"

"Brenda is not my wife," Joe interrupted. "She's not my girlfriend either. There should have been another person with us, but she's away on honeymoon, so Brenda and I agreed to share a caravan, on the understanding that she got the master bedroom, and I make do with the little playpen of the small twin room. It's an economic arrangement, saving us the cost of an extra caravan, but we don't sleep together, so Brenda can't corroborate my whereabouts in the early hours of this morning. But you should talk to your boss, Hattie. He's looking in the wrong direction, and while he's concentrating on me or Ava Garner, the real killer is sat back laughing at you."

Hattie finished her tea, stood up and put her coat on. "I think he knows that, Mr Murray. Thanks for the tea, I'll be around for the next few days, and if you learn anything, don't hesitate to let me know. Ritchie might not listen to you, but I will."

Joe's showed her out, closed the van door, and took out his laptop, booted it up, and began to make notes on what he had learned during the day. An hour later, the job completed, as he put the machine away, Brenda came out of the back bedroom, and promptly asked whom he had been talking to.

While never ceasing to marvel that she could look so good even after just crawling out of bed, Joe gave her a full account of his afternoon's efforts, and with the time coming up to half past six, he dug out his camera, and put his coat on.

Finishing a vital and invigorating cup of coffee, Brenda asked where he was going.

"Top of the hill, on the dunes. The sun sets just after seven o'clock, and I want to try and catch it."

"Give me a couple of minutes, Joe, and I'll come with you. I want to see this myself."

As always, Brenda's 'couple of minutes' turned into a quarter of an hour, before they stepped out of the van, shivering in the evening chill, and strolled up the lane towards the beach.

At the crest, from where they could look over the entire beach and bay, they met Sylvia Goodson and Les Tanner. Sylvia was well wrapped up, a woolly bonnet pulled down over her ears, a heavy coat buttoned up to the neck, and thick socks showing from the top of her sensible flat shoes. Tanner, too, was wrapped in a quilted coat, his head topped with a trilby hat, and he was busy fitting a lens to his Canon digital camera, and assessing the lighting.

Joe had a similar model (a Sony) back in Sanford, and he had brought only a compact digital.

"Just under twenty-five megapixels, Murray," Tanner boasted. "DSLR, came with two lenses, two batteries, and frankly the camera body cost more than your cheap little café makes in a day."

Joe held up his Nikon compact. "Sixteen megapixels, fits in your pocket, no faffing about, cost me a ton and a half, and at our age, you couldn't count the difference in pixels between the pictures I produce and those you turn out."

"Like dealing with two schoolboys comparing bicycles," Sylvia said.

Brenda agreed. "Or the size of their—"

"That's enough of that," Tanner interrupted.

Brenda chuckled. "I was going to say laptop screens, Les."

The sun appeared to accelerate as it dipped towards the

horizon, but then, invisible cloud, or perhaps some kind of atmospheric haze, began to distort the scene as Joe and Tanner snapped away with their electronic gadgetry.

"Any news on that poor girl?" Sylvia asked.

Unable to resist the temptation, Brenda said, "Twice they've spoken to Joe. The last time, he tried bribing them with tea and biscuits, but I still think they have him in the frame for it."

Joe responded without taking his eye off the tiny screen of his camera. "And if they pin it on me, it'll be a better frame than any I can put round these pictures."

Chapter Eight

Keith applied the parking brake, a loud hiss of air came from the bus; he left his seat, then turned and faced his passengers. Monday morning, and he was not in the best of moods.

"Right, crumblies, this is it. This is where we park for the day." He checked his watch. "It's half past ten, and according to Les, you want to be back at Gittings by five o'clock, so if you can all be back here by a quarter past four, we should be in plenty of time."

He reached back to his dashboard and pulled the lever to open the door.

Joe, as always, was first off the bus, and stood by to help those who were not so nimble.

They were parked in a layby on the road immediately in front of the main bus/car park of St Ives, which was set on a hill, high above the town.

"Are you okay parked here?" Joe asked.

Keith pointed at the yellow crosshatch markings on the ground, and up at the nearby sign. "It's a bus stop, Joe, and this is a bus, in case you hadn't noticed." He waved both hands at his vehicle. "But I can't stay here for long. I'll have to shift onto the official park, and pay the fee."

Joe looked around. The car park, already filling up with private vehicles, rose steeply away from them, while to the other side there was a fine view looking over St Ives and across the whole of Carbis Bay, but no matter which way he considered it, the route down to the town was steep, and he mentioned it to Keith.

"No choice, Joe. No way would I get through the traffic in the town centre. But you don't have to walk." He indicated the bus stop again. "There's a regular bus which'll take you down and bring you back. I don't imagine it'll be that expensive."

"I wasn't thinking of me," Joe said as he helped Irene Pyecock off the coach. "I can manage the walk down, and I could probably tackle the walk back up."

Keith was unrepentant. "Well, that's the situation. Besides, knowing these daft old sods, they'll be too drunk to walk back this afternoon."

"Count on it," Irene said as she stood to one side and waited for her husband.

Brenda stepped off the bus carrying Joe's rucksack, and paused to help Sylvia Goodson down.

"What's the rucksack for?" Keith asked.

"After what the cops told me yesterday, all my worldly goods are in it. Well, those worldly goods someone might choose to nick."

"Like your wallet?"

Joe turned superior eyes on their driver." I never tell anyone where my wallet is."

"Sometimes, he doesn't tell himself," George Robson said as he stepped off the bus. "Especially when it's his round."

"Take the words off and p—"

"Hey," Brenda cut Joe off.

He smiled mock-sweetly. "I was gonna say 'push'. You know. Push off."

Brenda cast a sceptical eye at him as she handed over the rucksack. Joe dragged it onto his back, and they crossed the road to begin the descent into the town.

"It reminds me of Whitby," he said while they walked down the steep path.

Brenda waved a sweeping arm at the vista before them, taking in the town and the calm waters of the bay beyond, glittering blue/green in the autumn sunshine. "No way is this anything like the Yorkshire coast. Just look at the sea, Joe. You couldn't swim in the sea off Whitby, even in the middle of summer."

"But you can in Filey," Joe argued. "Anyway, I didn't mean the sea, I meant the hills. Remember, we stayed on the headland at Whitby, and that's what this reminds me of."

He glanced over his shoulder where other members of their party were following them down the steep incline. Further back, as Keith moved the coach onto the main car park, he could see yet others waiting for the service bus. Considering the gradient, it made sense for the more elderly members; people like Sylvia Goodson and Irene Pyecock, while behind Joe and Brenda, George and Owen, Alec and Julia Staines and Mort Norris and his wife, appeared to have no difficulties with the walk, but like Joe and Brenda, they were still of working age.

A thought occurred to him. "I don't see Stewart Dalmer."

Brenda clung on to his arm as the gradient increased. She replied with the distraction of someone taking care not to slip and fall. "He's gone to an antiques fair in St Austell or Truro or somewhere. It's his business, Joe. You know it is."

"Yeah. I'm not bothered. But I did wonder is there something between you and him?"

The path ended at the top of a flight of steep steps, and as they began the descent, Brenda chuckled. "Jealous?"

"Am I hell as like." He removed her hand from his arm and encouraged her to take hold of the safety rail. "This way, if you fall, you don't drag me down with you."

"That's what I love about you, Joe. Always the gentleman. And to answer your question, mind your own business. It's nothing to do with you who I'm seeing."

Joe clucked impatiently. "What is it about women that they can take everything and put the wrong twist on it?" He paused to get his breath, and faced her. "I'm concerned for you, Brenda. I always have been. You and Sheila. I don't want to see you hurt by some guy who might just be using you to get his hands on your antiques."

Brenda laughed aloud this time. She leaned forward and pecked him on the cheek. "The only thing that is antique in my house is me, and he'll only get his hands on me when I let him. Now come on. All this walking is making me peckish. Let's get down to the town."

The incident had not gone unnoticed by those members

following them, and as George and Owen passed them, George commented, "Two-timing me, Brenda?"

"I've been two-timing you with everyone in Sanford, George."

"Except me," Joe added.

At length, weaving their way through narrow streets and lanes of stone-built houses, traditional fishing cottages, and larger buildings converted to high-priced apartments, they emerged onto the main street leading to the town, and five minutes later, they came upon the small bus terminus, where the service from the car park had just arrived. As they walked past, Sylvia and Tanner, the Pyecocks, and other members of the 3rd Age Club got off the bus, and while some waved, Tanner gave Joe a self-satisfied smile.

Joe was quick to take the wind from his sails. "Some of us still have it, Les, others don't."

The street narrowed further, familiar shops began to appear on both sides, and ahead, they had their first view of the harbour, no more than a glimpse of the path by the side of the slipway in the south-eastern corner.

"No thoughts on this dead woman, Joe?" Brenda asked as they emerged onto the harbour side, and looked around the long semicircle of shops and cafeterias.

"I don't think it's as clear cut as I first suspected," he replied. "Not after what Hattie O'Neill told me last night, when Charlie Curnow tipped me off that the girl was a bit of a vamp. I don't mean she was jumping half the park, but her bite was a lot worse than her bark."

"You suspect blackmail, obviously, and you reckon that's why she was killed?"

Ahead of them, George and Owen ducked into the first pub they came across. Joe and Brenda carried on walking, until they rounded the bend at the far end of the harbour, and then settled at tables outside a café. There was no waiter service, Joe took out his wallet, left his rucksack with Brenda, and went inside. He emerged five minutes later empty-handed.

"They'll bring the food out. I ordered sandwiches and tea."

Brenda nodded. "Good enough."

"You should see the prices. It's like armed robbery without the guns. If we charged prices like that, we'd be making a fortune, but we'd lose the Sanford Brewery boys, and the factory hands from across the road."

He settled into his chair and watched a middle-aged couple waving away the attention of seagulls.

"Scavengers," he muttered. "The birds, I mean, not those old duffers. What were we saying? Oh yes, Wynette Kalinowski. I've always said that your chief witness in any murder case is the victim. You have to know about him or her, and to be honest, Brenda, I know nothing about this girl other than what I've seen, and we both know that appearances can be deceptive. Eleanor Dorning didn't want to speak ill of the dead, Charlie Curnow didn't give a toss, and he indicated that she was not the sweet little innocent you might think. Howell and Hattie told me nothing about her, and without more to go on, I can't begin to guess. Blackmail? Yes, it's possible. Especially after what Winnie said to Charlie Curnow. But I need to know a lot more about her before I'm willing to commit myself."

The sandwiches and tea arrived, and they settled back to watch life and occasional members of their elite club, pass them by. Despite the hurly-burly of the previous twenty-four hours, Joe was in a relaxed mood, and if he had any regrets, it was that Maddy was not here to enjoy it with him. Brenda was good company, but after a brief fling in their teens, and an even briefer one later in life, they were in a position that Joe had always deemed impossible between man and woman; a genuine, platonic relationship. Brenda, along with Sheila, was simply one of his best friends.

Brenda's voice cut in on his ruminations. "I wonder how Sheila's getting on."

Joe often believed that the two women could read his mind. Had he not just been thinking of the absent third member of their triumvirate?

"She seemed all right on Saturday."

"Yes, but it's not right, Joe. She should be here, with us."

"She's married now. She has different priorities. Besides, we've never lived in each other's pockets, have we? Well, you and Sheila, maybe, but not me."

Brenda was still thinking about Joe's words, and was about to answer, when they were distracted by a disturbance further along the road. Two men burst from a takeaway, just a few doors along from them, and they were grappling, wrestling, trying to throw punches at each other, but so close that they could not connect. As people turned to stare at them, they sank to the ground, rolling around the sandy cobbles.

"If nothing else, they're scaring away the seagulls," Brenda said as she got to her feet.

Joe had recognised at least one of them, and was ahead of her. While others continued to stare, he and Brenda made an effort to pull the two apart, and compelled them to get to their feet.

Joe studied the face to his right, the one he had recognised as a member of the entertainments staff from the previous night. A rough beard clung to his tanned chin, connecting with his sideburns, and his long hair hung in an untidy straggle above the collar of his tatty combat jacket.

Joe also recognised the other man as a Gittings barman who had served him the previous night. Tidily dressed in jeans and a black fleece, clean shaven, his close-cropped hair also filled with sand and grit from the ground and his square chin jutting out, his eyes of tiny fire were concentrated on his opponent.

"Aren't you guys a little old for fighting in the street like schoolkids?" Joe rounded on the entertainer. "They call you Flick, don't they?"

"Why are you poking your nose in?"

Joe ignored the inherent threat in Flick's response, and faced the other. "What's your name?"

"Quint."

Joe tutted. "Flick and Quint? Do parents ever give their children proper names in this part of the world?"

Neither man chose to answer him, but Quint pointed a

shaking finger at Flick. "He killed. Winnie. Filled her with dope."

"You're talking out of your backside, *Quentin*." Flick stressed the final word as a taunt, and it occurred to both Joe and Brenda that Quint did not like his real name.

"I know all about you, *Frederick*."

Judging by the stress Quint placed on the name, Joe and Brenda felt the same could be said of Flick.

The childish teasing signalled another tussle, but before they could meet, Joe put himself between them, and held out his hands to stop them. They collided in the middle, almost crushing Joe, and Brenda had to drag Quint away while Joe, recovering quickly, pushed Flick back.

By now the incident was the centre of attention, crowds of people out for a day at the seaside, taking a vigorous interest in the fight.

With a good deal of irritation, Joe lectured the two men. "Take it from someone who knows, fighting solves nothing." He rounded on Quint. "Now what are you talking about, lad?"

With Brenda holding him back, Quint was restricted to waving a floundering, accusing arm at his opponent. "Him. I know what he gets up to. Selling stuff all over the park."

"Bit of booze and baccy, that's all."

Quint sneered. "Yeah. Wacky baccy, you mean."

Joe snapped his head round and glared at Flick. "You're selling drugs?"

"He doesn't know what he's talking about, pal. The only thing I ever filled Winnie with was me, and he can't stand it that she preferred me to him."

"Then ain't true, and you know it, Tolley."

Now Flick began to sneer. "Oh yeah? So how come she was hassling me for us to live together the night before she died?" He stared Brenda in the eye. "If anyone killed her, it was him, because he couldn't stand the idea of Winnie chucking him over for me."

The blood rushed to Quint's cheeks. "No way would she want someone like you in her life. You're scum, you are."

"I'm an entertainer, and so was she, and that's what she wanted. Someone who could look after her properly, and take an interest in her singing, not someone who knows how to pull a pint."

The argument could have gone on for some time had not Joe intervened. "The best thing you two can do is go your separate ways. Have either of you spoken to the police? Because if you haven't, you should. If you don't, they'll come looking for you."

Flick let defiant eyes rest on Joe. "Do a Winnie and drop dead." With that he turned and walked away.

Still alongside Brenda, Quint still looked hurt and angry. Joe waved at the nearby pub. "Doors are open. Fancy a drink, lad? Just to calm you down?"

Brenda took the young man's hand and led him into the bar. Joe followed, and while they found a table by the window, he paid for drinks, two halves of lager, one for him, one for Quint, and a Campari and soda for Brenda.

They settled into the table, he and Brenda facing the distressed young man. Joe pushed a glass of lager across to him. "Get that down you, china, and calm down a bit."

Through the window, he could make out Flick's tall figure stumbling away around the harbour side, hands thrust into his pockets, shoulders hunched, his gait spelling out bubbling anger. As he wandered along, he shouldered his way through crowds, drawing one or two angry glances.

Quint appeared more sad than annoyed. His shoulders were drooped, hands busy, playing with his glass, and when he raised it to his lips, he sipped, rather than gulping down the sparkling, amber ale.

"What's your proper name, son?" Joe asked.

"Quentin Ambrose." He delivered the news with a good deal of contempt. "Now do you see why I like to be called Quint?"

Brenda smiled. "It could be worse. We met one barman in Windermere those first name was Storm."

"That's parents for you," Joe said. "They don't always stop to think how their kids might suffer." He took a mouthful of ale. "All right, Quint. What was the crack between you and Winnie?"

"Is it any of your business?"

"I'm making it my business. Y'see, we already know she was murdered, and I reckon you know it too, otherwise you wouldn't be so mad. But it was a knife in the belly which killed her, not anything Flick might have sold her. You're sure he's dealing drugs?"

"Certain of it. I know he sells booze, hooky cigarettes and baccy, but he also sells coke, E, maybe a bit of H."

Brenda frowned. "And it is common knowledge?"

"No. A good few of us know, but Eleanor Dorning doesn't."

Joe's next question was more to the point. "Is Charlie Curnow aware of this?"

Quint shrugged and took a larger drink from his glass. "I don't know. He sells the smoke and booze, too, and for all I know, he could be supplying Tolley."

Joe backtracked a little. "Let's put that aside. I asked you what the score was between you and Winnie. Did you have something going down?"

"She was my girl until last season, when Flick turned up, and he turned her away from me. Not totally, though. She was still with me now and then, and I was willing to settle down with her. I told her that lots of times this season."

"Did you see her at all Saturday night after the show was over and the bar was closed?"

"Yeah. We was on our way back to the staff vans, and I told her I still wanted her. She said she had something to sort out and she'd catch me later." A tear began to form in his eye. "That was the last time I saw her. Next thing I knew, Eleanor was telling us all she'd been found dead on the beach." The anger began to return to his voice, and he clenched his fists into tight balls. "That Flick. He killed her. I know he did."

Chapter Nine

It was a pensive Joe who climbed off the bus when they got back to Gittings.

When Quint left them, they spent the remainder of the day wandering round the attractive and crowded little town, Brenda did some 'upmarket' shopping, and Joe picked up one or two souvenirs; a tobacco tin with a cartoon sun shining over St Ives, a reproduction watercolour of the harbour, which would hang on the wall in his flat, and a map of 'Arthurian' Cornwall which he declared to have less basis in genuine history than Sanford's role in winning World War Two.

"At least our boys dug out some of the coal."

He planned to hang it on the wall of The Lazy Luncheonette.

Overrunning her monthly budget, Brenda bought a couple of tops, and a pair of white and pale green, flower-patterned, casual pants, elasticated at the waist and ankles, of which Joe, with his usual candour, declared, "Too noisy and too tight across the bum." The moment he expressed his dislike, Brenda paid for them.

Eventually, as was almost inevitable, they came to the Tate St Ives, and after a brief debate, turned and walked away. Joe never considered himself ignorant of art, but neither was he a connoisseur, and Brenda insisted that she would only go into the place if Sheila were with them.

They took a light lunch at the harbour side: genuine Cornish pasties, bought from a shop close to the café where they had had morning tea. Joe chewed through the crust, savoured the meat and vegetable filling, but ultimately declared his preference for steak and kidney pudding. Brenda ate barely half of her pasty, and inevitably the seagulls of St Ives feasted on the discarded remains. Breaking up the pies and throwing bits for the birds drew frowns of disapproval from people who Joe imagined were locals or regular visitors. There were signs all around asking people not to feed the seagulls.

Throughout the afternoon, Joe was noticeably quiet, mulling over the information Quint had given them, and assessing the possibilities and probabilities, and Brenda finally called him to order when they sat on the harbour side of the sea wall, overlooking the Atlantic Ocean beyond the calm waters of the bay.

"I miss Sheila," she admitted, waving at the serene picture before them. "I can't relax properly without her, but what's worse I can't draw you out. Not when she's not here. What is it, Joe? Those kids we were dealing with earlier?"

Joe took his time rolling a cigarette, lighting up and then sitting back to let the calm of the warm, autumn day and the fine view of the sea and sand wash over him. He took a second drag, let the smoke out with a soft hiss, and watched the light breeze take it away.

"Like you, I'm probably missing Sheila. I would have preferred Maddy to be with us, too, but we don't always get what we want, do we?"

"Is it getting serious? You and Maddy, I mean?"

He puffed again on his cigarette and shook his head as he blew out the smoke. "If anything, it might be tapering off. Neither of us wants to be tied down, Brenda." He gave her a wry smile. "I don't need to tell you what that's about, do I?"

"No, you don't. The only reservation I have is how will I feel in ten years' time? I always figured you, Sheila and me would grow old together, but it's not to be, and, no offence, but I don't see myself growing old with you."

Joe laughed at her good-natured, albeit honest response. "No offence, and none taken. If it's any consolation, I feel the same about you. You're a smashing woman, Brenda, but if we set up home together, it would be world war three in a matter of days."

Silence followed, and for Joe it was a long impasse, allowing the gears of his agile mind to mesh and turn over the events of the last forty-eight hours.

"You're hard work sometimes," Brenda said. "I left my mindreading skills at home, so you have to tell me what you're thinking."

"I'm thinking about Quint and Flick. Quint reckons Flick is selling drugs on the park. It wouldn't surprise me. Cornwall may be a tourism heaven, but according to my best guess, it's an employment vacuum, and such work as is available, is probably low paid. Let's face it, drug dealing is common in places like Sanford, where we have better employment prospects, so I reckon it would be just as common here, and if that's so, Gittings won't be exempt."

Brenda took a moment to absorb the information. "Let me see if I get your drift. If Flick is dealing drugs, Winnie could have threatened to turn him in, and that might prompt him to get rid of her. Yes?"

Joe nodded. "That's one angle, but there is another."

Brenda raised her eyebrows. "Elucidate."

Joe stared at her, his eyes wide open. "Elucidate? Where did you find that word? On the back of a cornflakes box?"

She chuckled at his ribbing. "The second angle?"

"Quint. You could see it in his face. He loved that woman, and we both know that love is a more powerful emotion than hate. She rejected him… Or at least, that was his view. It was there to be read in his eyes when he was talking to us. What price he followed her to the beach, begged her to reconsider, and when she told him where to get off, he lost the plot, thought 'if I can't have you, no one can', and knifed her?"

Brenda's face spread in amazement. "Good God. I never thought of that, but it's so obvious when you do." She spent a minute looking out to sea again, as if seeking inspiration, and then faced her long-time friend and boss again. "Should we be telling Sergeant O'Neill this?"

Joe, too, gazed out to sea, but his eyes were glazed, as if he were not taking in the magnificent view. "That's the sixty-four thousand dollar question, Brenda. I don't wanna make life difficult for these people, the police or the crew at Gittings, but that girl was murdered, and you know my opinions on that. No one has a right to take another's life, and if they do, then they should pay for it. Unfortunately, that tends to create a lot of flak for other people around them. Remember Holgate in Torremolinos? Innocent people were hurt in the process of exposing him; people like Josie Keeligan and Sandra Greenwood."

Brenda nodded. "And the guy who ran that bar, Coyote's. What was his name? Paul Wylie? Him whose wife was fooling around with George Robson."

Joe echoed her nod. "We're in the same situation here."

"We always are. Whenever there's a murder. How many alleged innocents did you hassle during the treasure hunt in Whitby? How many people did Sheila and I upset with that business at Squires Lodge? It goes with the territory, Joe, and you can't avoid it. You should tell Sergeant O'Neill what Quint told us. Hell, for all we know, she may already be aware of it."

Joe crushed out his cigarette on a nearby stubber, and got to his feet. "I'll have a word with Eleanor Dorning first, see what she has to say."

"And get them the sack whether they've done anything wrong or not?"

"I'll keep their names out of it."

***

They were amongst the first to arrive back at the coach at a quarter to four, and as they settled into their seats, Joe picked up his Ian Fleming paperback, Brenda settled for her MP3 player and a lifestyle magazine.

When the local bus arrived, many of the club members got off, and made their slow way up the steeply sloping car park to get on the bus, and as Keith had predicted earlier in the day, some of them were worse for wear for an afternoon of drinking.

Everyone was back on board just after four o'clock, he

climbed into his seat, started the engine, and rolled gently out of the car park, following the signs for Hayle.

Joe found it impossible to concentrate on the novel. The fresh information from Quint played upon his mind, and no matter how hard he tried to dismiss it, he could not. Wynette Kalinowski's death preyed upon him, the way so many murder cases had done in the past.

Experience told him that even the most complex murder cases boiled down to quite simple motives, and it was just as likely that Winnie had been murdered by Quint in a fit of jealous rage, as Flint covering up his purported illegal activities. Not only Flint, but Charlie Curnow too. There was nothing alleged about Charlie's crimes. He was smuggling – if that was the correct word – contraband goods and selling them quite openly, and it was with some chagrin that Joe recused himself on being a party to that crime. Like any businessman, he cut the occasional corner, but The Lazy Luncheonette did not deal in stolen or contraband goods. Everything bought as stock and sold in the café went through the books.

With a curious counterpoint, he felt absolutely no guilt at having bought cheap tobacco from Curnow. Joe's weak argument was that if he didn't buy it, someone else would, so he might as well take advantage of it.

When they got back to Gittings, by which time many of the passengers had to be woken from half-drunken sleep, Joe left the task of helping others to Brenda and Les Tanner, while he hurried across to Reception and asked to speak to Eleanor Dorning.

In stark comparison to many other people, she seemed to be genuinely pleased to see him, greeting him with a warm, generous smile, but when Joe asked if she could spare a few minutes, she had to (politely) decline.

"I'm on duty until eight o'clock, Joe, and I can't get out of it."

She looked good, smartly turned out in her company uniform with its dark blue, knee-length skirt, close-fitting, white shirt which accentuated her bustline, and the blue and red, patterned neckerchief.

Joe glanced around ensuring that none of his fellow members were nearby. "Well listen, Eleanor, how about I buy you dinner. Not here. Somewhere a bit better, a bit more, er, upmarket, shall we say?"

Joe was difficult to embarrass, and in common with many other people from Sanford, he did not mince words, but having posed the question, his ears began to colour at the awful realisation of having asked this woman (several rungs up the social scale from him) for a date. He anticipated rejection, but to his surprise, Eleanor's smile broadened.

"That would be wonderful. Can I meet you here, say, quarter past eight? I know a little place just outside the town. Quiet, pleasant atmosphere and excellent food."

Joe beamed. "It's a date." His smile faded. "Collar and tie?"

"No. They're not that fussy, but if you're dressing casual, they do like smart casual."

"Quarter past eight. I'll be here."

He was almost skipping like a teenager as he made his way back along the accommodation lines to his shared caravan, where he found Brenda setting up her laptop in preparation for a call to Sheila.

"You're looking pleased with yourself," she commented without taking her eyes off the task at hand. "What's up? Have you found a shilling?"

"Better than that."

"Half a Crown then?"

"Even better than that, and before you mention money again, I've got a date."

"Right, Joe." Brenda concentrated on her laptop screen, accessing the wi-fi, logging on and opening up Skype. "I hope Sheila and Martin aren't… What did you say? You've got a date?"

Joe nodded and pulled a chair up alongside her. "You'll have to get Stewart Dalmer to look after you in the bar tonight. Eleanor Dorning is taking me to a local restaurant."

Brenda pursed her lips demonstrating how impressed she

was. "Proper little Lothario, aren't you. Maddy Chester at our end of the country now the park manager at this end, what are you gonna do when we go to London?"

"I'll probably pull one of the servants from the palace and end up with an OBE. Now are we talking to Sheila or what?"

The connection was difficult to establish, but at length they found themselves looking at Sheila's paled features in the centre of the laptop's small screen. Although she looked pleased to see them, there was a hint of emptiness behind her smile, and it took a little while for Brenda to find out the cause.

"Dicky tummy."

"You've been drinking the local water, have you?"

Sheila denied Brenda's accusation. "Bottled water all week, I promise you. It must be something I've eaten."

"Does Martin have the same trouble?"

Joe's question had to be repeated after the wi-fi connection broke and a minute or two passed before they could reconnect, at which point, Sheila told them that Martin was fine.

"We've had different meals, and anyway, he has a stronger stomach than me."

She went on to assure them that she was still enjoying the break, but she was missing them as keenly as they missed her. They exchanged pleasantries on Sheila's hotel and Gittings Holiday Park, and it wasn't long before Brenda, having run out of inconsequential conversation, told her of Winnie Kalinowski's murder.

Sheila was shocked, and after another wi-fi breakdown, she narrowed a disapproving stare on Joe, and went on to ask whether he was poking his nose in. Joe denied it, but he did so tongue in cheek, and Sheila scolded him for his failure to relax.

Joe dismissed her complaint. He was looking forward to a date.

Shortly before eight o'clock they stepped out of the van, locked up, and made their way towards the entertainment centre, but Joe veered off into Reception when he saw Les

Tanner gesticulating wildly at one of the counter hands.

"I'll just go and see what's going on," he said to Brenda.

She carried on towards the main building, and Joe continued to Reception to find Tanner, his face flushed a furious red, haranguing Eleanor and one of her female assistants.

"What's the matter, Les?"

Tanner rounded on Joe. "My camera is the matter, Murray. It's been stolen."

Joe laughed nervously. "What? And you're accusing these people?"

Tanner's rage increased. "I'm accusing them of employing thieves."

"Just calm down," Joe advised. "The way you're ranting, you'll have a stroke. Did you not have the camera with you in St Ives?"

"No. I locked it in the caravan. I didn't want to lug it around the town, and I assumed it would be safe there. I've obviously misjudged this place and the efficiency of these people." His blazing eyes cornered Eleanor. "If you knew anything about management, this kind of thing wouldn't happen."

She made a strenuous effort to appease him. "I can only apologise, Mr Tanner, but company policy makes it clear that we cannot be held responsible for property left in the accommodation. Naturally, I'll fill out a report, and ensure that it's passed to the police, but I don't know what else I can do. You must be insured?"

Tanner's rage barely subsided. "That camera cost me a better part of a thousand pounds, and of course I'm insured, but no amount of money will replace the photographs I've already taken."

"Well, as I say—"

"Your apology is not good enough, madam. Rest assured, I will be submitting a formal complaint to your head office."

Joe, keen to ensure that Tanner's fury did not blight the evening's prospects, intervened. "For crying out loud, stop being an old woman, Les. You can't hold these people to ransom for your irresponsibility. Leaving the camera in the caravan was a bloody stupid trick. Even if you didn't want to carry it round St Ives, you could leave it on the bus. For all his moaning, it would have been safe enough with Keith."

"I never considered you particularly pleasant or dependable, Murray, but I never expected to see the day when you would side with strangers against me." With that, Tanner stormed from the building and marched, stiff-backed, to join Brenda and Sylvia Goodson outside the entrance to the show bar.

Joe gave Eleanor a sickly smile. "Sorry about that. I hope it doesn't change our plans?"

Obviously relieved to see the back of Tanner, she returned the smile. "No. It's fine, Joe. If you give me five minutes, I'll finish off in here and meet you outside."

Chapter Ten

According to Eleanor, The Smugglers Inn was poorly named.

"This part of Cornwall was never popular with smugglers," she explained. "So far inland there isn't enough sand and there are too few coves."

It was a cosy, stone-built pub/restaurant on a narrow road between Hayle and Penzance, less than fifteen minutes' drive from Gittings.

Joe was less interested in the place's name than the ambience, which he found perfect for a discreet tête à tête. The lighting was low, the tables were arranged in booths which enhanced their privacy, the background music was set at a volume which allowed conversation, yet prevented others eavesdropping, the staff did not pester them, and while Joe was none too pleased at the exorbitant prices, the food, when it arrived, was as good as Eleanor had promised.

They both rejected starters, and while Eleanor opted for a vegetable quiche, Joe's conservatism favoured a char-grilled rib-eye steak, and when it came, he gave it top marks.

"Not something I normally say about cooks… other than myself, naturally." He smiled broadly to hint that he was joking, and Eleanor returned the smile.

They kept the conversation neutral. Joe had questions which he needed to ask, but he was anxious to avoid spoiling the convivial atmosphere, at least until the meal was over.

She asked how his day had been, and he told her of their visit to St Ives, eliminating reference to the fight between Flick and Quint. Returning the query, he asked about the long hours she appeared to work.

"It's not as bad as you may think, Joe. I'm on what's known as a split shift this week. Talk to any bus driver, and he'll understand what I mean. I started at eight, worked until twelve, and then took four hours off, while my assistant took over. She was working ten until six, and I came back on duty at four. It's a way of ensuring that there is a senior manager on duty throughout the day."

"Interesting. So what do you do with your four hours of free time? Nip home and catch a nap?"

She giggled through a mouthful of quiche. "Home is a caravan on the site. I live there for most of the year. I do have another place in Truro – technically my mother's old house – but living on site saves me the commute every day, and it also means I'm handy for emergencies."

At the mention of 'emergencies' Joe was tempted to dive into his vital questions, but he resisted the urge, and pressed her a little further.

"So you went back to the caravan and caught up on a bit of kip?"

"Normally, yes, but not today. I went to a flea market in Truro. It's a regular thing, and you never know what kind of curios you might pick up there."

Joe's eyes lit up. "Oh. One of our members is an antique dealer. Stewart Dalmer. I wonder if that's where he went today."

"Probably. I don't know of any other second-hand markets in Truro." She chuckled again. "I hope he had more luck than me. I didn't find anything that took my fancy."

"He knows his stuff," Joe commented through a mouthful of steak and vegetables. "And the same could be said of this chef. The steak is excellent."

At the end of the main course, Eleanor chose a fruit salad for dessert, and Joe ordered a slice of lemon meringue pie with fresh cream, and once again he was full of praise for the restaurant.

When the meal was over, he ordered coffee and after-dinner mints, and spent a few moments rolling a cigarette (only to be advised by the management that if he wished to smoke, he would have to step outside) and considered his approach.

With the drinks delivered, he tucked the cigarette in his pocket, and leaned his elbows on the table, playing with his cup and saucer. "This isn't all about asking you out, Eleanor. I don't wanna spoil the evening, but there are matters I have to bring up with you."

She gave him the tiniest of nods. "Your friend's camera?"

"What?" Joe was momentarily flummoxed, and then recalled the argument between himself, Eleanor and Les Tanner. "Oh, no. I don't give a toss about his camera. If the bloody fool hadn't left it in the caravan, it wouldn't have gone missing. No, no." He was silent for a moment. "There was an incident in St Ives today. Two of your staff fighting outside a takeaway."

Her pleasant features became more serious. "Which two?"

"Flick. I remember him being one of the entertainments staff last night. The other is a barman whose proper name is Quentin, but who likes to be called Quint."

Eleanor's features darkened further. "They were arguing about Winnie, weren't they?"

Joe agreed and gulped down some coffee. He unwrapped an after-dinner mint, and went on, "Quint made some fairly serious accusations against Flick. Drug dealing."

It occurred to him right away that he was not telling Eleanor anything she did not already know, and she confirmed as much.

"I'd be very surprised if there was no dealer at Gittings. It's par for the course these days. It's common in towns and cities, and almost inevitable that someone on the site will be selling drugs, and we do get droves of young people staying during the summer. But to be honest, Joe, I'd need a lot more than Quint Ambrose's accusation before I could instigate any proceedings." She sighed. "I suppose I could call in the police, but Flick would deny it, and I can't have them searching every van on site. It would upset too many of the holidaymakers. I need firm evidence. Has anyone – Flick or anyone else – offered you anything?"

"No." Joe felt a rush of guilt with the memory of buying contraband tobacco from Charlie Curnow. He chewed on his mint and swallowed it. "If they did, they'd get a mouthful, and I would bring the matter to you. I'm not afraid of naming names, Eleanor. Never have been. You know Flick better than me. Is there any danger that Quint is right?"

She shrugged and sipped her coffee. "Your guess is as good as mine. I wouldn't call him shady, exactly, but he is a bit... What's the word... Irreverent. He doesn't care much what people say or think about him. I can tell you that he and Wynette were a couple. They were not living together or anything like that, even though Winnie's ambitions might lie in that direction, but I do know they were sleeping together occasionally."

Joe was surprised. "And you don't mind?"

"I don't know what I can do about it. Theoretically, we have a rule which forbids crew members of the opposite sex sharing a caravan, unless they're married, but it happens. I know for a fact it does, and to be honest, there's no practical way of stopping it, other than fencing off the male and female caravans and putting guards on them. But we're a holiday park, not a concentration camp, and our security people have more important duties than looking out for couples getting it on."

Eleanor drank more coffee and chewed delicately on an after-dinner mint. Her face was serious, contemplative, as if she were trying to work out a more definitive answer to Joe's question.

At length she asked, "Can I ask how this accusation came about?"

Joe, too, had to consider his words. "I'm not sure you really want to know."

"Oh but I do."

He took a deep breath. "Quint accused Flick of murdering Winnie because she threatened to expose his drug dealing."

The reaction was as he had expected; total shock. "That is serious."

"As serious as it gets, but is it possible? Is Flick the kind of man who would be ready to commit murder?"

His question was followed by another long silence during

which she weighed the possibilities and formulated an answer.

"Off the top of my head, I would say yes. Flick is a hard nut. Try calling him by his proper name, Frederick, and you'll see what I mean. You caught them fighting. Chances are that Quint accused Flick and he reacted. Not that Quint is incapable of looking after himself," she hastened on. "He's worked behind the bar at Gittings for the last five or six years, and like any other bar, we get occasional aggro. Quint knows how to deal with it, and if it comes to blows, he's not afraid to trade punches."

"He doesn't like his given name, either, does he?"

"No. Getting back to your original question on Flick, I wouldn't describe him as a cold-blooded killer, but it wouldn't be beyond him if he lost his temper, and if he's dealing drugs, and if Winnie threatened to expose him, then yes, I can see him jamming a knife into her tummy." She tried to smile. "Sorry, Joe. A lot of 'ifs' in that summary."

Another piece of information which Joe slotted into his compartmentalised mind. "And what about Quint? Could he have killed her in a similar fit of temper?" He leaned forward, stressing his next point. "You see, it was obvious to me – and my friend, Brenda – that Quint was in love with the girl."

"Everyone knows that. Winnie was his girl until Flick arrived last season." Eleanor became more pensive. "Could he have killed her? I shouldn't have thought so, but I really don't know."

"But you can understand what I'm getting at?" Joe urged. "Madly in love with her, she rejects him, and he loses the plot. Yeah?"

Eleanor forced another wan smile. "You're not exactly preaching to the choir, I'm afraid. I've never been married, and even if I'm no stranger to relationships, I've never had one I felt that strongly about."

"Me neither."

The conversation came to a halt, and it was followed by a diffident silence, which Eleanor broke.

"Is that it, Joe? Is that all you wanted to ask me?"

"No. There is one more issue, and this one came from Sergeant O'Neill. I suppose it touches on the business with Les Tanner, but she told me that Gittings, in common with a few of the holiday parks in the area, suffer an awful lot of thefts from the vans, and she – and the police in general, I suppose – believe it's down to your cleaning contractors."

He expected the question to annoy her, and he was pleasantly surprised by her non-reaction.

"She's exaggerating, Joe. Yes, we get thefts, yes we tend to look at the contractors rather than our full-time staff, all of whom we vet thoroughly before we employ them, and yes, I know it's a problem on other parks in the Hayle, Penzance, St Ives area, but it's not as prevalent as Sergeant O'Neill makes it out to be. It's occasional incidents, like the one with Mr Tanner, but she makes it sound like an epidemic."

Joe was still walking on egg shells when he asked, "So it's not something that Winnie would be involved in?"

Eleanor shook her head. "I told you, we vet our employees thoroughly. Winnie had no criminal record, and if she was involved, then I'm disappointed in her." A deep frown crossed her features. "But I can't see how that would be a motive for murder."

"That depends on whether you've had a thousand quid's worth of camera nicked."

Eleanor's hand flew to her mouth. "You don't think Mr Tanner—"

Joe cut her off with a hearty laugh at the imagery the unfinished accusation generated in his mind. "Les Tanner? Knifing a girl? He's too much of a gentleman. He'd at least say to her, 'excuse me, madam, but would you mind turning your back while I kill you'." His laughter echoed around their booth and beyond. "Captain Les Tanner is a toy soldier. A member of the Territorial Army Reserve. The nearest he comes to killing anything is when he pours weedkiller on his flowerbeds." His laughter subsided and he sobered up. "No, I was thinking more of thieves falling out, but if you tell me she wasn't involved in that kind of thing, then I accept that.

Course, she could have tumbled who the thieves were, and decided to bubble them." He held up his hand and signalled a waiter. "Anyway, let's forget it all for now. Eleanor, it's been a smashing evening. I'll just get the bill, and we can be on our way."

She reached for her purse, but Joe held up a hand to stop her.

"I'm the biggest tightwad in Yorkshire, but when I take a woman to dinner, she keeps her money in her bag." He grinned. "Anyway, I'm not in Yorkshire, am I?"

He left his seat, visited the smallest room, then settled the bill, and while Eleanor also visited the toilet, Joe stepped outside to smoke the cigarette he had rolled.

Notwithstanding the debate over Wynette's death and the level of theft on the park, it had been an excellent evening, so much more invigorating than sitting in the bar watching his fellow club members playing bingo, followed by hick entertainment by a bunch of wannabes led by a has been.

And it was not over. When Eleanor returned, they climbed into her car and she pulled off the car park. Turning left for Hayle, she asked, "Would you fancy a nightcap?"

He was happy to agree. "Another pub? A ceilidh? Or are you thinking of Gittings' show bar?"

She smiled secretively. "Somewhere a little more, erm, exciting."

Joe's pulse quickened. Was there something hidden in the invitation? And what was behind that secret little smile?

Women were a mystery to him, but beyond that their interest in him was an even bigger mystery. He did not consider himself good-looking, and standing barely 5'6", he would be hard pressed to dominate any situation by raising himself to his full height. In fact, just like many other women, Eleanor was taller than him... without shoes. He had no reputation as a Romeo, and he was notably timid in asking women for a date, let alone persuading them to take matters further.

Neither was he an intellectual. All right, so he could solve the cryptic crossword in the *Daily Express* most days, he was not bad with medium-difficulty sudokus, and he had a basic understanding of psychology, which often helped identify the motives of a criminal, but talk about art, genuine philosophy, advanced maths, astronomy, a whole host of subjects, and he was a virtual Neanderthal. He knew nothing.

As a businessman he was shrewd with an innate ability to maximise profits, thanks largely to his negotiating ability, but many men would have put such talents to use making their first million. Joe was comfortably off, but he was nowhere near a millionaire, and the size of his empire was restricted to The Lazy Luncheonette, which was unlikely to get him on the front page of *Time* magazine as man of the year. As far as he could recollect, he had never made the *Sanford Gazette's* shortlist for the town's person of the year.

And yet, now and again, he would meet a woman like Eleanor who for some inexplicable reason was attracted to him… at least, he hoped that was the reason behind her invitation. His inbuilt early-warning radar was never engaged when he entertained the company of such a woman, as a result of which he would never dare make the first move.

Consequently, it was an uncharacteristically jittery Joe who followed Eleanor into her van set amongst the staff accommodation and away from the lines of guests' vans.

The layout was standard, but she had done much to turn it from a 'place to crash' into a home. China ornaments were ranged along the shelves, photographs stood here and various scents, none of which Joe could specifically identify, drifted from bowls of potpourri set at strategic locations.

Eleanor took two brandy balloons and a small bottle of Courvoisier from an overhead cupboard, and poured a small measure into each glass. Handing one to Joe, she made herself comfortable on the long settee beneath the window, and curled her legs up under her, which had the effect of making her skirt ride up above the knee.

Joe averted his eyes, sipped his brandy, and racked his brain for something to say. If ever he needed small talk, it was now, and as always, he had none, other than the stalwart, tedious British standby of the weather.

He needn't have worried. Eleanor had plenty to talk about, including the recent Women's World Cup and the political upheaval across Europe. Joe commented as best he could, even though he was not aware that there had been a Women's World Cup.

And throughout her chatter, he sneaked occasional glances at his watch, and finally, with the time reading 11:30 p.m., he finished the brandy, got to his feet, and said, "Ah, well, time I was getting—"

He never finished what he was going to say. With a speed that alarmed him, Eleanor leapt to her feet, rushed across the van, threw her arms around him, locked her lips to his, and pressed him back onto the opposite settee.

Joe was not certain whether to feel relief or more apprehension, but he succumbed to the moment…

Chapter Eleven

When Stewart Dalmer stepped out of the bedroom and into the kitchen at nine o'clock the following morning, Joe was chewing his way through a bowl of cereal.

Dalmer appeared embarrassed. "Oh. Good, er, good morning, Joe."

Joe made an effort to be friendly. "Morning, Stewart. I saw your jacket hanging on the door, and tried to keep the noise down when I came in last night."

It was an edited version of the truth.

At her insistence, he left Eleanor just before one in the morning.

"Discretion, Joe. It would be brilliant to have you spend the night here, but I can't afford for anyone to see a guest leaving my van in the morning." She had smiled coyly at him. "But if you want to knock on the door after lights out tomorrow…"

She had left the suggestion in the air, and Joe came away a happy, satisfied man, moreover, one who had satisfied a demanding woman, with the promise of more to come in twenty-four hours.

When he got back at his own caravan, he picked up the sound of bedroom activity as he opened the door, and it was noticeable that the van was rocking slightly on its rear suspension. After his own lascivious exertions, he could hardly frown upon Brenda's activities, so he pottered quietly around the sink, making a cup of tea, and crept into his bedroom, waiting for the bumps, moans and groans coming from the next bedroom, to subside.

The caravan was designed so that Brenda had a toilet in her room, so he was not disturbed by either her or Dalmer attending to their post-coital ablutions. And he knew it was Dalmer. He really had spotted the brown leather windjammer hanging behind the door when he first came in.

Notwithstanding the time he went to bed, Joe's inbuilt alarm clock woke him at half past six. He nodded off again, but finally rose at half past seven, washed and shaved, dressed, and stepped outside for the first cigarette of the day while watching the growing daylight.

There was no sign of cloud in the sky, and it did not take long for the chill to nip at his arms. The lights were on in the Staineses van next door, but there was no sign of Alec, so without any further distraction, after smoking a cigarette, he went back into the van, and switched on the gas heater.

He passed an hour updating his journal with the events of the previous day, including non-salacious references to the evening and later hours spent with Eleanor. His primary concern now was the murder of Wynette Kalinowski, and he made a mental note to chase up Sergeant O'Neill before the day was out. Beyond that, the 3rd Age Club had no plans (although they were scheduled to visit Penzance on the Wednesday) and as far as Joe was concerned, there was nothing on the horizon other than pottering about on the park, or maybe going down into Hayle for the day.

Dalmer switched on the kettle and reached up into an overhead cupboard for a cup. Only then did it occur to him that he needed to ask permission. "You don't mind, do you, Joe?"

"Help yourself, mate. You're Brenda's… Brenda's guest, aren't you?" Joe had been about to say 'Brenda's lover' when he checked himself. "I believe you were in Truro yesterday."

Dalmer fussed at the kettle. "Yes. Second-hand market. Well, you know it's my business, and frankly, you never know what you might pick up at these places."

"I suppose so. Find anything interesting?"

"As a matter of fact, yes. I picked up a book for ten pounds. The story of HMS Amethyst. She was shelled by the Chinese when she came down the Yangtze in nineteen forty-nine, you know. The father of a friend of a friend was a crewman aboard the Amethyst. Lost a leg in that particular action. I thought I might be able to sell the book on. Make a small profit. You know."

Joe finished his cereal and pushed the bowl to one side. "That's what business is all about." He took a swallow of tea. "Eleanor Dorning, the general manager here, was on the same market apparently."

Dalmer collected his cup and saucer and joined Joe at the table. "Really? Can't say I noticed her. Mind you, it was very busy."

"All antiques?"

Dalmer smiled. "Hell, no. It's a bog standard flea market. You can buy just about anything there, including an ancient Amstrad computer if you wanted one. And some of the traders were selling bits and pieces that weren't exactly old. You'd be surprised at the number of mobile phones you can buy on the stalls."

The comment reminded Joe that no one had mentioned anything about Winnie's mobile, and he made a mental note to ask Sergeant O'Neill about it.

"You were missed in the bar last night." Dalmer sounded diffident, almost as if we were reluctant to bring up the point.

Joe shrugged. "I had a date. It's not illegal, you know, Stewart. I'm a single man, over twenty-one, and I can go out with whoever I please. I was with Eleanor Dorning, and it turned out to be a spectacular evening. That's when she told me she was on the same market as you. Did you and Brenda get far last night?"

Dalmer shook his head. "We had a meal in a pub in Hayle, then came back here for the alleged entertainment. To be honest, I'm not that impressed with the shows, and that comic, Curnow, sails a bit too close to the knuckle for my liking."

"He's old hat."

The pass door to the bedroom opened, Brenda emerged, dressed in jogging pants and a thin, woolly top. She dropped a benign smile on Dalmer, and a cynical scowl on Joe.

"You remember where you live then?"

Joe could not help rising to the challenge. "Yes. Do you remember what you said when I brought up the subject of sharing a caravan? It amounted to me having to make myself scarce, so I did."

She obviously had no more to say to either of them, and when she had made herself a cup of tea, she moved to the far corner and switched on the television.

While she watched morning TV, Joe engaged Dalmer in a deliberately animated conversation concerning HMS Amethyst.

It didn't take long for the lecture (for that is what Dalmer turned it into) to wind down, and at half past nine, he packed his rucksack, put on his fleece, and bidding them 'adios', left the van.

Joe had worked with Brenda long enough to recognise her moods, and she was obviously in no frame of mind to entertain him. She had something on her mind, something she did not want to say in front of Dalmer, but which Joe guessed would be a brutal opinion about him. And for the life of him, he could not think what he might have done to upset her. It would be something trivial, he had no doubt. Probably something to do with Sheila's absence. Whatever it was, he had more on his plate than Brenda Jump's sensitivity, and she would almost certainly catch up later in the day.

He wanted to hire a car, and Reception was a logical place to ask, but as he made his way there, he was uncertain that it was a good idea. Eleanor had said she was on split shifts all week, so she would be working at this time, and he was not sure how he was supposed to deal with her after their adventures last night.

He diagnosed it is another symptom of the one area in his life where he remained uncertain: women. He did not want Eleanor to think he was badgering her, or worse, stalking her, but on the other hand, he did need a set of wheels.

Thanks to Alec Staines, he was saved the trouble. As he reached the entertainments complex, Alec pulled up in a hired car, and although Joe did not get the chance to speak to him (Julia climbed into the car when Alec stopped, and they drove away) he nevertheless made a quick note of the hire company's telephone number, as displayed on a small banner in the rear window. Ten minutes later, he had booked a compact Citroen for the next three days, and was waiting for a taxi to take him into Hayle where he could collect the car. Once arranged and paid for, he settled behind the wheel, activated the satnav, and found his way to the police station, only to learn that it was shut. He called up the Internet on his smart phone, and checked St Ives and Penzance, and once again learned that they were not manned twenty-four hours. In fact, he would have to travel to Camborne in order to contact Sergeant O'Neill.

He recalled that she had given him her card, and digging it from his wallet, he rang her.

"Nice to hear from you, Mr Murray, but we're quite busy right now. Is it urgent?"

"Urgent-ish. I just want to pass on one or two things I learned in St Ives yesterday."

"Can you ring me later? We're on our way to Gittings right now, but will be busy when we get there. Try again later this afternoon."

"Will do."

Joe killed the connection and sat behind the wheel of his hired vehicle. The heat of the sun, magnified by the windows, began to burn him, and he wondered what to do with himself. Brenda would not come out of her mood until they were alone, and she could speak freely, and he had no desire to hang around Gittings all day. At length, he called up Land's End on the satnav, fired the engine, and began to follow the route.

It was not complex. The A30 ran all the way, but as opposed to the broad trunk road the bus had followed from Exeter, in places it was not much better than a side road winding its way across bleak and barren moorland, then well-tended, agricultural land, and Joe had to wonder how the summer traffic, which would be far heavier than he was meeting, coped. Now and again, he had a fleeting glimpse of the sea to his left. He passed occasional, isolated farms and small hamlets, then drove sedately through the village of Sennen, took a fleeting interest in the First and Last Inn, and less than half a mile beyond a sweeping right-hand bend, he came to the imposing white buildings of Land's End.

Or rather, he came to the official car park.

It was not busy, but he had not expected it to be, and amongst the few cars parked there, he recognised the Vauxhall Corsa Alec and Julia Staines had driven off in… or rather, he mentally corrected himself, a Vauxhall Corsa exactly the same as the one the Staineses had hired, and from the same, Hayle company.

He rolled a cigarette, let the window down and lit up. It seemed to him that he had come quite a distance, but on checking the satnav while he enjoyed his smoke, he learned it was actually less than twenty miles.

Land's End had always loomed large in his mind as a special place, just like its opposite number, John O'Groats. It was the last outpost of England, the British Isles and beyond the rocky cliffs there was nothing for thousands of miles but open water. It was a romantic notion, but completely false. The Isles of Scilly lay only about thirty miles off the southwestern coast of Cornwall, and beyond them, the thousands of miles of Atlantic Ocean could be covered in a matter hours aboard a modern jet.

Joe had been here before, many years ago when he was with Alison, but he did not remember the white-stone and glass building, or indeed the security post where the guard directed traffic into the car park. He did, however, remember the wind, and when he climbed out of the car, ensuring he had his wallet, camera and tobacco, he hastily zipped up his fleece against the biting breeze. The sun blazed in the southern sky, but it could not compete with that seaborne wind.

He spent a few minutes ambling round the complex of gift shops and cafés, then emerging at the rear, made his way towards the First and Last House, a hundred yards away. Somewhere, in one of his old albums, he had a photograph of him and Alison sitting on a bench at the rear of the place.

He took a few photographs of the place and of the views over the sea, and the Longships Lighthouse a mile off the coast, then ambled back to the main visitor area. He was in need of a cup of tea.

He was hardly surprised to find Alec and Julia Staines in a café, and they welcomed him pleasantly enough, inviting him to join them. He bought fresh tea for them and himself, and sat down.

"Brenda out and about with Dalmer, is she, Joe?" Alec asked.

He shrugged. "I don't know. She's not talking to me."

Alec chuckled. "Doesn't surprise us, does it Jay?"

Joe had known them both for over half a century, and in all that time, he had never seen Alec lose his temper or even get into a flap. His business was at least as successful as Joe's, and he and his wife (a woman Joe had designs on back in their late teens and early twenties) shamelessly enjoyed the fruits of his solid reputation for dependability and craftsmanship.

When their son Wes had been accused of murder on his wedding day, Alec had remained calm personified, but Julia had been close to hysterical. Even now, while she frowned at her husband, Alec showed no sign of emotion other than affability.

He responded to Alec's last observation. "You're not surprised? How come?"

"You mean you don't know?"

"Now Alec—"

Staines shushed his wife, and raised his eyebrows at Joe, who replied with his customary irritation. "No, I don't know. What's going on?"

Obviously aware of what was to come, Julia excused herself. "I'll just go to the toilet."

Alec watched her leave, and then focussed on Joe. "Les Tanner, mate. He's called an extraordinary meeting for five o'clock this afternoon."

Joe was amazed. "What? While we're away on holiday? Has the power gone to his head or something?"

"He's asking the members to boot you out of the 3rd Age Club."

"He's what?" Joe curbed his initial flash of temper. "All because of his bloody camera, I'll bet."

"Probably."

Joe considered the proposition, forcing his anger to the back of his mind so he could concentrate properly. "I don't think he can do it. Not while we're this far from home."

Alec drank tea as he shook his head. "Yes, he can. Theoretically. The quorum is only fifty, Joe, and there are seventy of us on the bus." He put his cup down. "He won't do it, mind. I won't vote with him, neither will Julia, Brenda won't, obviously, and I'm certain George and Owen won't back him. Even Sylvia has argued against it."

"I should think so. Hell, I founded the club, me and Brenda and Sheila, and he and Sylvia were amongst the first people we approached, along with you and your wife, and George and Owen." He fulminated in silence for a moment." And what am I supposed to have done?"

"You took that woman's side against him. Her you were jumping last night."

"So it is over his damn camera. Wait while I see him."

Through the glass door, Alec could see his wife making her way back. He finished his tea and stood up, ready to leave. "Be cool, Joe. He won't get away with it, and even if he did, when he calms down in a coupla days' time, he'll only rescind the decision. I'll catch you later."

Joe was left at the table fuming. Tanner's actions were the ultimate insult, and someone, he promised himself, would pay for this.

Chapter Twelve

Joe's anger was such that he had no desire to see any of his fellow club members, but he would have to face them, and he knew that he could not argue with any conviction while he was fuming. He needed to calm down.

He decided that a long, leisurely drive would solve the problem, and his first port of call was the souvenir shop where he bought a tourist's guide to Cornwall, and when he left Land's End, he took a more extravagant route back, turning off to the left as he bypassed Penzance. Following the satnav, he called first of all at the Merry Maidens stone circle, just outside the town, where he parked the car, wandered into the field and took several photographs of the standing stones from different angles.

From there, using his smartphone and the satnav, his journey took him north-west across the moors, in the direction of Zennor. He paused to take photographs of Lanyon Quoit, and his next port of call was Mên-an-Tol, a stone with a circle carved out of the middle, which from the proper alignment, allowed the viewer to look through the hole in the middle and see an erect, standing stone several yards beyond it. He took a photograph from the appropriate angle, with the thought that the sexual connotation was a little too obvious, and on returning to the car and researching it, he learned that it had a history of various theories and interpretations, only one aspect of which was concerned with fertility.

Driving along the lane back to what passed for the main road (but which was not much wider than the rough track he had just come from) he turned right towards the northern coast, and eventually joined the main road to Zennor. He stopped and enjoyed a cream tea at a roadside place, then, a further half mile on, he came to the remains of Carn Galver Tin Mine and its engine house.

He grew up in the coalfields of West Yorkshire, and was accustomed to the standard appearance of mines, with the familiar, girder structure of the wheelhouse. This was more picturesque, built of stone, and it's tall, stark chimney reminded Joe more of the woollen mills in Leeds and Bradford than the familiar pitheads of Sanford, Pontefract, Doncaster and Barnsley.

He finally got back to Gittings at half past three, and after parking the car alongside his caravan, he went in search of Les Tanner, only to learn from Mort Norris, that Tanner, along with Sylvia Goodson, Dalmer and Brenda, had taken a leaf from his book and hired a car.

"They've gone somewhere called Portperrin, Joe," Mort assured him, "and from there they're going on to Newquay."

Joe automatically translated Portperrin as Perranporth, and decided to make his way back to the caravan and wait for them to return. Eleanor intercepted him as he passed Reception.

"I'm sorry to bother you, Joe, but we have a bit of a situation."

"Yes, so have I. What's the problem?"

"The police are interviewing Flick Tolley. He's been in there an hour or more now, and I think they're going to arrest him."

Joe was not unduly troubled by the news. "For Winnie's murder?" Eleanor nodded, and Joe shrugged. "Can't say I'm surprised. I spoke to O'Neill this morning, and told her I had news. Maybe she won't need to speak to me now."

"I'll let them know you're here just in case," Eleanor said. "You won't forget tonight, will you?"

Joe had never been reminded of a proposition so blatantly, and he suppressed the urge to laugh nervously. "After lights out, you said? Does that mean after the show is over?"

"A little before, if you don't mind missing Charlie's spot. The whole of the staff will be busy in the show bar, and no one will be any the wiser."

"Half past ten, then?"

"Great."

Joe felt a noticeable spring in his step as he made his way back to the caravan, drank a cup of tea, and then settled down for an hour's sleep on the settee under the window.

Forty minutes later, a knock on the door woke him, and he opened it to find Sergeant O'Neill standing on the steps.

"Sorry to bother you, Mr Murray, but Inspector Howell would like a word. We're in Reception when you're ready."

Joe agreed to come along, and she left. He made for the bathroom and swilled off in cold water, washing away the day's fatigue, and then spent a minute rolling a cigarette before putting on his fleece and stepping out of the caravan.

Once outside, he sauntered along the lane, taking his time, enjoying the afternoon sun and the bite of tobacco on his lungs. Anything to keep Howell waiting. He did not like the inspector and it was obvious that the feeling was mutual.

He reached the reception area to find Eleanor pacing outside the office and smoking. She was relieved to see him, crushed her cigarette out on the wall stubber, and said, "This is awful. They're charging Tolley with Winnie's murder."

Joe shrugged. "They must have evidence. Howell might be obnoxious, but he's not stupid."

Eleanor chuckled uncertainly. "Sorry, Joe, I wasn't thinking about Tolley. I was thinking about Gittings, and the damage this might do to our image."

There was a time when Joe would have disapproved of such an attitude, but with a developing relationship (if that was the right word for libidinous fun and games) in mind, he confined himself to a wry smile and wagged a disapproving finger. "At a time like this, Eleanor, our thoughts should be with Winnie. I don't care who she was, what she was like, she didn't deserve to die like that."

"Of course not. Sorry."

"You don't have to apologise to me."

A car turned into the park and passed Reception. A quick glance at the Vauxhall saloon revealed Stewart Dalmer at the wheel, Brenda in the passenger seat, Sylvia Goodson and Les Tanner taking up the rear seats. Joe deliberately turned his back, and took Eleanor's hand, then led her back to Reception, cocking a childish snook at them. When the car was past, he released Eleanor's hand, offered no explanation, stubbed out his cigarette and stepped into Reception, where Hattie O'Neill escorted him into a small, rear office.

Howell was in no better mood than he had been on Sunday. His tie hung from an open collar, he fidgeted with a ballpoint pen, and his face was a mask of frustration and irritation.

He glared at Joe, and barked, "Sit down, Murray."

Joe glowered back. "What are you gonna do? Feed me a *Good Boy* choc drop?"

"What the hell are you on about?"

Joe took a seat facing the inspector. "You're treating me like a dog so the least I can expect is some kind of reward for good behaviour."

"Just shut it. You're in trouble, so don't wind me up any further or I'll book you."

Joe was not impressed. "I'm in trouble, am I? You're walking on eggshells, Howell. Now explain yourself."

The inspector relaxed visibly, as if he welcomed Joe's challenge. "We've just taken Frederick Tolley in on suspicion of Wynette Kalinowski's murder, and it was thanks to information we received, information you were in possession of, but which you failed to pass on to us. That, Murray, could be interpreted as obstructing the police in the course of their enquiries."

Joe remained unfazed. "It could also be interpreted as the police talking out of their backsides, but there's nothing new about that, is there? It doesn't matter where I go in this country or Europe, I come across the same situation. You're still not explaining yourself, man, so let me hazard a guess. You've been listening to Quint, haven't you?"

Howell frowned. "Who?"

Joe was equally puzzled. "The guy Tolley was fighting…" He trailed off. The look on Howell's face told him the inspector had no clue about the previous day's fight. "Well, if not him, who?"

Howell consulted his notes. "Sergeant O'Neill had a call from one Brenda Jump this morning, and she told us of an incident in St Ives yesterday. The only names she mentioned were Frederick Tolley and Quentin Ambrose. According to her, Ambrose accused Tolley of murdering Ms Kalinowski. Mrs Jump maintained that you were there, and not only witnessed the incident, but helped keep the two men apart. Yet you didn't see fit to report it. Why"

Joe's annoyance diverted along a path which led to Brenda. He put it to one side, and replied to Howell. "I didn't ring you because I tend not to pass gossip on. I know how misleading it can be. Ambrose, who, by the way, likes to be called Quint, was getting his hair off, nothing more. Fact is, he had just as big a motive for murdering Winnie. He was in love with her, and from all I can gather, she didn't return his feelings." He pointed an accusing finger at the inspector. "And you shouldn't be charging Tolley without some kind of evidence."

Howell shook his head in mock amusement. "You really think we're that stupid? Of course we have evidence." He leaned forward, fixing Joe's glare with his own. "When we questioned Tolley, he admitted getting into an argument with Kalinowski the other night, but he insisted that an argument was all it was. But, as you were told at the outset—" Now the inspector's glare transferred itself to Hattie O'Neill. "—there were finger marks on Kalinowski's neck. Those dabs match Tolley's. We figure he held her from behind with one hand gripping her neck, and then stabbed her. She didn't die on the beach either. She was stabbed on the dunes, and while she was dying, he lifted her onto his shoulder, and carried her down to the beach. It might also interest you to learn, Mr Smartarse private investigator, that when our people searched the dunes this afternoon, they found blood spatters amongst the grasses. Too early to confirm that it's Kalinowski's blood, but it seems pretty conclusive to me."

"Well, it would, wouldn't it? I don't want to tell you your

job, Howell, but if Tolley did it, there'll be traces of her blood somewhere on his clothing. Have you found it?"

"Not yet, but his clobber has been taken away for examination, and our forensic bods are going through his caravan with the proverbial. He did it, Murray, and I'll nail him for it, and you should be thankful I'm not charging you."

Joe shrugged. "If he did it, he did it, and there's no more to be said, but I've seen this happen before. Police moving too quickly and without conclusive evidence, and the next thing you know is a copper with egg on his face and an innocent man taking a chunk of next year's budget in compensation." He stood up. "The last time I saw it happen was to me." He turned on his heels and marched from the room.

He had barely made the door of Reception when Hattie caught up with him. "Mr Murray, please, wait a minute."

Joe paused outside the door, took out his tobacco tin and began to roll a cigarette. "What is it?"

"Like the inspector said, sir, we're not stupid. And just to correct you, we haven't charged Tolley. We're holding him on suspicion. Ritchie did say that."

He lit the cigarette and casually noticed several of his members making their way into the show bar. He suffered a coughing fit. Getting it under control, he dipped into the pockets of his fleece, and took a puff from his inhaler. Putting that back in his pocket, he took another drag on the cigarette much to Hattie's confusion.

"You're smoking yet you rely on an inhaler?"

"It's because I'm an idiot, but don't let that fool you, Hattie. It's the only area of my life where I'm an idiot. The thing that worries me is your boss's tunnel vision. He has his sights fixed on Flick Tolley, and he ignores everything else. I'm not saying you have it wrong, but if you have, the real killer is sat back laughing his socks off at you."

"I know that. That's why I want to talk to you."

Joe noticed Mort Norris, Mavis Barker and Cyril Peck heading to the show bar, and a quick glance at his watch told him that Tanner's extraordinary meeting was about to start.

He turned his attention back to Hattie. "Talk to me about

what?"

"Quentin Ambrose." She paused a moment following his eyes as he watched his fellow club members disappear into the entertainment centre. "Do you have somewhere you need to be?"

Joe shook he said. "No. If I go in there, I'll end up losing my temper. What is it you want to know?"

"You said Ambrose was in love with Wynette. It's the first we've heard of it."

"Now there's a surprise." Joe suppressed further sarcasm. "Sorry. That was uncalled for. Listen, Hattie, down the years, I've stuck my nose into a number of cases like this, and without exception, I always find there's more than one person with a motive. Tolley was goading Quint yesterday because Winnie preferred him. That set Quint off again. When Tolley stormed off, Brenda and I took Quint into a bar, and it was obvious that he was hopelessly in love with Winnie. I don't know anything about your track record, but as I said to Brenda yesterday, when it comes to motive, love is much more powerful than hate. If you have Tolley's prints on her neck, then fair enough. He must have grappled with her, and it's possible that he killed her, especially if, as Quint claimed, Tolley was dealing drugs and she threatened to expose him. But it's just as likely that Quint was watching from nearby, and when Tolley left, he killed her. Trust me, you need to speak to Quint Ambrose."

Hattie was busy taking notes, and as Joe finished speaking, she put her notebook away. "I'll make sure I tell Ritchie."

Joe tried to imagine the scene on the dunes, the argument, the struggle and the blade sinking into her flesh. "Have you identified the murder weapon?"

"Breadknife, we think. Sharp, with a serrated edge. Thrust in under the rib cage and upwards. Pierced the heart. She died almost instantly. The boss thought a hunting knife at first. You know. One of those you use for gutting. But the pathologist said the blade was a bit more, er, bendy than that, and not as broad. He suggested a bread knife." Hattie shrugged. "Know how many of those there are on this camp?"

"Hundreds?"

"Possibly thousands." She smiled. "I'd better get on. Enjoy your evening."

"That's not likely. While you're here, can I bring up another matter? A friend of mine had his camera stolen while we were in St Ives yesterday. It's an expensive model. Top range Canon, worth about a grand."

"Mr Tanner?" When Joe nodded, Hattie went on. "He's made us aware of it, Mr Murray, we did advise him to take better care of his property. Especially something as valuable as that. He should have taken it with him. On the other hand, he knows his own property better than anyone else, and he should keep an eye out amongst the second-hand dealers in this area, just on the off chance that it turns up."

Joe smiled broadly. "Exactly what I told him. Thanks, Hattie. You will let me know how you get on with Quint?"

"Count on it."

Chapter Thirteen

In a corner of the show bar, the air was thick with argument and counterargument.

In the absence of Sheila, the club's official secretary, Brenda had agreed to keep the minutes of the extraordinary meeting, but from the outset it was plain that the members were unhappy with Tanner's tough call for unpalatable action. Along with Joe and Sheila, Brenda had founded the club and she could not remember any member having been disenfranchised.

If she had any qualms about the way she had ignored Joe first thing in the morning, they were dispelled when she saw him take Eleanor's hand outside Reception, and any misgivings concerning the call of an extraordinary meeting were also dismissed.

But it was not a feeling that was shared by the majority of the members, as was obvious from the poor attendance. Less than thirty people turned up so, before Tanner began speaking, Brenda felt it necessary to point out that without a quorum, no firm decisions could be reached.

The captain did not let that hold him back, and launched into a scathing attack on Joe and his 'blatant disregard' for the welfare of his fellow members.

"I'm aware of Murray's history, and the way in which he established this club, but it's obvious that he's lost interest. And that's not just this week, but stretches as far back as our visit to Palmanova. My feeling is that if that is to be his attitude, then he should forfeit the right to membership."

His haughty and pontificating manner did not go down well with the attendees, and one of the first people to speak up was George Robson.

"What you wanna do is get the pole out of your arse."

Tanner's colour rose, and George took obvious satisfaction from it.

"That's hardly the kind of language one expects to hear at a formal meeting."

"Meeting? We're on a holiday, man. What kind of idiot calls a club meeting while we're away from home?" Tanner would have interrupted, but George pressed on with his attack. "So Joe's scored, trapped off. What about it? More power to his elbow, I say, but you're not kids, none of you. If you hadn't been so gormless as to leave your camera in the caravan, it wouldn't have been nicked."

Glad of the chance to intervene, Tanner responded by going on the attack himself. "You think it's just my camera, do you? I'm not the only one to have something stolen." He waved a hand at the small audience. "Norman here is missing a gold pen."

Norman Pyecock nodded. "Presentation pen from the firm where I were working when I retired. I've had that pen a good few years."

"Aye, and I'll bet it's still in Sanford, you daft old sod."

George's acid remark provoked a round of accusation and counter accusation, and some forcibly expressed opinions from Pyecock and Tanner, the former insisting that he had used the pen the day before to write a postcard for his grandchildren.

Tanner called the meeting to order, and detailed other thefts, particularly Mavis Barker's MP3 player, and an iPad stolen from Mort Norris's caravan.

Eventually, notwithstanding the questionable validity of a vote, Tanner called for a show of hands on the revocation of Joe's membership. Sixteen people were in agreement, including Brenda and Stewart Dalmer. Thirteen disagreed, amongst whom were George Robson and Owen Frickley, and Alec and Julia Staines.

At the conclusion of the business, Tanner insisted, "When we get back to Sanford, I'll be calling another meeting, and open the issue up to a larger share of the membership."

The meeting began to break up, and Brenda and Dalmer

joined the Staineses.

Alec was no more nor less laid back than usual, but he laid a disapproving eye on Brenda. "I'm surprised at you voting against Joe, Brenda. Haven't you calmed down yet?"

"I voted for the club, Alec, not Joe, and the reason I did so is because he no longer cares about the club."

Julia was more disapproving of her husband. "Just because he's poking his nose into a murder? He's done that for as long as we've known him."

Alec pressed the point further. "One of those suspects he helped clear was you. Gibraltar Hall. Remember? *I Spy*?"

"I haven't forgotten, Alec, but that was a different Joe."

"Yes, well, we haven't heard his side of the argument have we?"

"And do you know why?"

"Because he wasn't told of the meeting," Julia said. "Well, not officially, he wasn't. Alec and I told him when we saw him at Land's End this morning, but he wasn't given any official notification, was he?"

Brenda was scathing. "No, he wasn't, but that's because he wouldn't answer his phone. I tried to ring him half a dozen times today, and I couldn't get an answer. To get back to what I was saying, the reason we haven't heard his side of the argument, the real reason he didn't attend, is because he was holding hands with his new girlfriend outside Reception when we drove past."

Dalmer nodded judiciously. "You've just said, Alec, Julia, that he knew. If it was of any importance to him, he would have made the effort."

"Say what you like," Alec declared, "but I won't desert him. Never. If he took this woman back to Sanford, threw the towel in, and dropped the club of his own accord, I'd still back him." He stood up and while he waited for Julia to join him, he laid an uncharacteristic glare on Brenda. "That's what you do for friends."

Brenda watched them march away, and turned her sad features on Dalmer. "Are they right? Am I just being childish and spiteful?"

The antiques dealer shrugged. "That's a question only you can answer. Frankly, I'm with you. I think Joe is looking for fresh horizons, and I also think that you should maybe keep your distance… at least until we get home."

"We share a caravan, Stewart."

"You do, but I don't. There's plenty of room in my van, Brenda, and you're more than welcome to stay with me. And I'm not angling after anything in return."

Brenda chewed her lip. "I'll think about it."

***

Passing through the show bar in search of Charlie Curnow, Joe noticed the group of Sanford 3rd Agers in the far corner, and ignored them. Other than Alec Staines telling him, he had not been formally invited, so he was not interested in anything they might have to say. Even the quickest of glances, however, was enough to confirm that there were considerably less than fifty people in attendance, so whatever Tanner tried to push through could not be ratified.

It was still a source of indignation and irritation for him. He'd given the better part of a decade to the club, and for them to turn on him like this was (in his eyes) the ultimate treason.

He pushed through the double doors at the bottom end of the room, and into the backstage area where Curnow and the remaining members of the entertainment team were rehearsing a complex dance routine. A CD player stood on the trestle table where he had last spoken with Curnow. The volume was reduced so it could not be heard out in the auditorium, but it was loud enough for the team to hear.

The rehearsal was not going well. Using a remote control, Charlie stopped the music, and ranted at his team. "You lot are a waste of my time and energy. My old drill sergeant would have had you all on fatigues for the next week. Now for crying out loud…" He trailed off noticing Joe. "What the hell do you want? I'm busy."

"I can see. But I won't keep you long. Just one or two questions."

"Didn't I tell you to clear off the other day?"

"You did, but I'm like a bad penny. Come on, Charlie, the filth have arrested Flick, but I'm not certain he did it."

Curnow turned to his team. "All right. Take ten, you lot." He led Joe to the trestle table, and sat down.

"You were in the army?" Joe said taking a seat opposite.

"Seventy-seven to seventy-nine. Royal Marines." Curnow patted his rotund belly. "I was younger, slimmer and fitter in those days."

"You didn't stay in for very long did you?"

"Dishonourable discharge."

Joe chuckled. "Bootlegging booze and ciggies?"

Curnow nodded. "What do you want?"

"I told you. Plod have arrested Flick. You're the man in the know. You know your team better than anyone. Is it possible?"

Curnow sighed. "Probably. Possibly. I'll make no bones about it, Murray, Flick was a tough cookie. He acted as a runner for me. He picked up the gear in Penzance and Falmouth, and he got a good dip out of it. I'm gonna need to replace him." Curnow yawned. "It won't take that much doing at this time of year. Plenya blokes looking for extra dosh. Why do you care?"

"Because over the last few years I've been arrested twice on suspicion of murder. The first time was a woman I was dating, and the second time was when the crook who burned down my café, turned up dead. Both times, I was innocent, but I remember what it felt like. Howell insists he has evidence, but it all sounds a bit thin to me, and there's at least one other suspect. How much do you know about Quint Ambrose?"

Curnow sneered. "Mummy's boy. Him murder Winnie? Do me a favour. She'd make porridge of him."

He reached into a side drawer, took out a bottle of Irish, unscrewed the cap and poured a generous slug into a beaker. He offered the bottle to Joe who declined with a shake of the head. Dropping the bottle back in the drawer, Curnow took a swallow, and asked, "What put the filth onto Flick?"

"Quint."

Joe went on to describe the confrontation between the two men in St Ives, when he had finished, Curnow laughed cynically.

"Flick? Dealing drugs? Never in a million years. I'm not saying it doesn't happen, but there's no way he has the brains to get involved in anything like that. He already has a record, but it's mostly for thieving and fighting."

"You seem to know a lot about him considering he's only been here for two seasons."

Curnow ran his hands from shoulder down to knee. "I might look like a sad sack of spuds, but don't let my appearance fool you. I'm the entertainments manager because I know my stuff. I take these jerks on." He nodded backwards towards his dancers who were kicking their heels, waiting for his return. "I audition them, and I say yea or nay, and I want to know everything about them, and we do check out their criminal convictions. When I get anyone with a serious record – like drug dealing – I don't take them on. That's it in a nutshell. If you want to look at anyone dealing drugs on this park, don't look at my crew. The bar staff, the maintenance people, even the cleaners, but none of my people. Now is that it? Only I have to get these muppets ready for tonight's show, and I'm without my two leads."

Joe prepared to leave. "Is that a big problem?"

Curnow shrugged again. "Not so's you'd notice. I already have a warbler to replace Winnie. Dorinda. Didn't you see her last night? Oh, course you didn't, you were too busy giving Eleanor what for between her sheets, weren't you?"

Joe felt a shock run through his heart, but there was no point denying it. "How do you know about that?"

"Nothing escapes the people in this place, pal." Curnow downed the rest of his Irish. "Y'see, there are two communities on the park. You and us. You're a bunch of strangers, to us and each other, but we're like any other bunch of waifs, strays, scroats and vagabonds. We look out for each other. Sneaking into her van before the end of our set and sneaking out again at one in the morning doesn't mean you don't get noticed, and like any other close community, word soon spreads." The comedian grinned. "What are you worried about? People know, but it doesn't mean they give a flying one. And do you think you're the first? Well known for letting her drawers down is our Eleanor." He laughed at Joe's glum face. "What's up? Got a wife hidden away somewhere?"

"Ex-wife, and she's not hidden. She's in the Canary Islands. Thanks for your help."

***

The first people Joe bumped into as he left the show bar were George Robson and Owen Frickley, who had encouraging news for him.

"Tanner was left looking a right berk," Owen said. "Sixteen for, thirteen agin, but he's threatening to call another vote when we get home."

Joe could not be less interested. "Let him. I've just about had enough of him… and others."

George took the hint. "You mean Brenda? She's only narked cos you didn't take her to bed."

"I offered," Joe lied and George laughed again.

"What chance have you got when I'm here?" George went on more seriously. "Worst thing you did was hand over the club to that nit-picking prat, Joe. Anyone'd think he owns it."

Joe was not in a communicative mood when he began the walk back to their respective vans, and despite the efforts of his two old friends, he preferred his own company. He thanked them and they went their separate ways.

"A different man," Owen commented. "Ever since that woman of his, that Denise, was killed."

Inside the van, Joe might just have agreed. His head was swimming with the things he had learned during the course of the day, and he could not make his mind up which to prioritise; the events at Gittings or the way in which Les Tanner and the 3rd Age Club were trying to ostracise him.

When it came to the former, the case was wide open (even though the police had taken Tolley in for questioning) and as far as the latter was concerned, he could not decide whether to feel sorry for himself or angry with Tanner… and Brenda. Her attitude was especially annoying considering their long years of close friendship.

Brenda returned to the caravan a little after half past seven, and although she was reluctant to speak to him, she made it clear that she had come, to change into her evening clothes. "I'll be staying with Stewart for the rest of the week."

Joe did not reply, and she disappeared into the rear rooms. Ten minutes later, she emerged wearing a dark top to match her black pants, and as she prepared to leave, she stopped and turned angry features on him.

"Just to bring you up to speed, if you're at all interested, Norman Pyecock, Mort Norris, and Mavis Barker have all had things stolen from their caravans.

Joe grunted. "Maybe they'll learn not to leave them lying around in future, then."

He did not look at her when he replied, and that, plus the acid in his response, only exacerbated Brenda's anger. She left the caravan and slammed the door behind her.

Joe did not leave the van until much later. He microwaved a frozen meal, and passed the hours in speculative thought centred mainly on his future. A few minutes after half past ten, he knocked on Eleanor's door, and she let him in. It was obvious from his glum face that there was much wrong, and when she asked, Joe found he could pour his heart out to her.

"There are people in Sanford I can still count on, but not many, and to be honest, Eleanor, I'm thinking of chucking it all in, and moving permanently. I have friends on the Yorkshire coast – well, one friend at least – and I have contacts in Tenerife."

"It would be a brave decision, Joe. Especially at our time of life."

He noticed that she was careful to stress 'our time' rather than 'his time'. And that diplomacy was maintained when she subtly reminded him that he was not there for counselling, but to satisfy their need of each other, and by eleven o'clock, he had forgotten anything other than that need.

Chapter Fourteen

Wednesday morning was the start of a busy forty-eight hours for the Sanford 3rd Age Club. A scheduled shopping trip to Penzance would be followed on Thursday by a much longer journey to Tintagel.

Although no one had any objections to Penzance, several people had raised questions on the advisability of the fifty mile journey to Tintagel following on so quickly, but Tanner had stressed that the alternatives were to either cancel one of the excursions or reschedule Tintagel for Friday, but that would mean a tiring, 100-mile round trip on Friday, followed by an even more exhausting 400-mile journey home on Saturday. In the end, the members agreed to deal with the excursions on Wednesday and Thursday, which would give them Friday to recover.

In light of the antipathy some members had for him, Joe had all but decided to skip both excursions, but when he awoke on Wednesday morning it was with a sense of grievance which gave rise to ardent defiance. He had been looking forward to Cornwall for months, and he was damned if he would miss even the simple shopping trip, never mind the myth of Tintagel.

Consequently, he was amongst the group waiting for the bus just before ten o'clock on Wednesday morning, and the only concession he made to the other members was to stand apart from them while he enjoyed a cigarette.

His normal seat on the bus was the front row on the opposite side to Keith, the driver, but there was a jump seat just inside the door, and in view of the irritation between himself and Brenda, he lowered that and strapped himself in for the half-hour journey.

Their driver gave him a curious look, but passed no comment. A fair number of the members ignored him, but in what he suspected was a show of support, George Robson, Owen Frickley and the Staineses all bid him a cheery 'good morning', and as if to demonstrate her absolute impartiality, Sylvia Goodson did likewise, much to the annoyance of Tanner.

The situation was untenable, and he knew it would need to be brought to a head, but that was more likely to happen in Sanford. In the meantime, he had three more days of this angry impasse, four if he counted the full day's journey home on Saturday.

He had said as much to Eleanor the previous night.

After their mutually satisfying exertions in the bedroom, she had taken a quick shower, and asked him if he would prepare toast. He obliged, but with appalling mental images of Wynette Kalinowski filling his mind, he was reluctant to use the breadknife to cut slices from the loaf, and instead chose a meat knife.

Over tea and toast before leaving her, he spelled out the situation between him and the members in greater detail, and Eleanor urged patience.

"Friendships are like that, Joe, even long-term ones. I'm sure they'll see sense eventually."

Joe was not so certain, and after making arrangements to meet again on Wednesday night, he made his way back to his van and spent an uncomfortable, largely sleepless night alone.

It was not an unfamiliar situation. Had Sheila been with them, he would have been alone anyway, and back home in Yorkshire, he lived alone. The antidote was the Miner's Arms where he could mingle with his friends, most of them members of the club, and without the unfortunate turn of events, he could have mixed with those same people here in Cornwall. They did not want him, and because of that same hostility, he did not want them.

He could not recall any time in his life when he had been so isolated. Even when he ran from the murderous intentions of a crazed killer in Palmanova, he was alone for only forty-eight hours before hooking up with his ex-wife, Alison. And when he left her, it was to join Maddy on the Yorkshire coast. Joe Murray, proprietor of The Lazy Luncheonette, may have been irritable and outspoken, but the social Joe Murray was a different man, and his current segregation grated upon him.

Penzance was a bore. Aside from souvenirs for Lee, Cheryl, and young Danny, there was nothing he was in need of, and he spent much of the day wandering up and down Market Jew Street, the main shopping area. He called in at the local interest centre, and learned some of the history of the town, but nothing of the curious name of the street. Not because it was not available, but because it did not occur to him until much later in the morning, when he was taking lunch at a café on the raised sidewalk halfway down the street.

After lunch he continued to troll up and down the street, checking out this shop and that bargain store, this fashion emporium, that mobile phone centre, and as he passed a shop going by the curious name of Entiex, it's banner declaring 'branches all over the southwest' he paused to look in the window.

It was one of those places which specialised in buying and selling second-hand electronic equipment: mobile phones, tablets, cameras, electronic games and such. He was tempted to go in and check on the price of iPads, but he changed his mind. If something went wrong, it was too long a journey to bring the machine back. Instead, he doubled back, and ambled through the Waterside shopping centre until he came out by the harbour.

He spent an hour in a nearby pub in the company of George Robson and Owen Frickley. They were heavy drinkers, and while Joe could not take alcohol in such amounts he found the company at least warm and welcoming, and when Charlie Curnow stepped into the bar, he at least gave brought a little light relief with him.

Curnow stood a round of drinks, and over the next thirty minutes, kept them chuckling with jokes, many of which were older than Joe.

Just before he left, Curnow asked, "Are the filth any further forward with Flick?"

Joe shrugged. "You tell me. It's not like they keep me informed."

"But you still think they've got it wrong?"

"No. Not necessarily." Joe was happy to have something to talk about other than his problems with the 3rd Age Club, and tackled the subject with gusto. "All I'm saying is, there's more than one suspect, and they should be looking at Quint Ambrose too. You ever been in love, Charlie?"

The question drew smirks from George and Owen, and a roar of laughter from the comedian.

"Yes. With myself." More soberly, he went on, "I was married, but it was a marriage made in hell. I should have guessed, really. When we flew off on honeymoon, she was the pilot, and the plane was her broomstick."

Joe nodded sagely. "Been there, done that. Not quite as bad as you make it out, but it didn't work."

"Our marriage was fine," Curnow went on, "but she couldn't stand the never-ending stream of jokes, especially since most of them were about her. I mean, I'm not saying she was ugly, but when she walked into the bathroom, the mirror turned its face to the wall."

George and Owen laughed heartily. While not especially politically correct, Joe had always considered gags based on appearance or body shape to be demeaning, and he smiled thinly, and only then to avoid an inevitable inquest.

Curnow sensed his discomfort, and when he brought the subject back to Quint Ambrose, Joe credited the comedian with the innate wisdom of a long-term stage performer, able to sense when the audience, or part thereof, was not on his side.

"So what were you saying about love?"

"I said it yesterday. It's much more powerful than hate, and in my book, it makes young Quint as likely a suspect as Flick. The only thing against Flick are his finger marks around Winnie's neck, but, you know, it doesn't make sense."

Curnow frowned. "Why?"

Joe shook he said. "I don't have all the details, so I don't know, but it all depends on handedness. The way Hattie O'Neill says Winnie was stabbed was under the rib cage and into the heart. That means she was stabbed on the left hand side. There are two ways Flick could have done that. He either held her from the front using his left hand, and then jabbed the knife in using his right hand, but holding her in that position, she would have been backing off. If he was holding her from behind, as Howell says happened, he would have needed to put his right hand on her neck, and then reach round her and jabbed the knife in upwards, but it would be an extraordinarily lucky shot, because from that angle, he wouldn't be able to see what he was doing. You see what I mean?"

Curnow considered the proposition, and responded, "It could be that he held her by the neck and pressed her to the ground before stabbing her."

Joe pursed his lips. "Possible, but neither Howell nor Hattie mentioned anything about a larger area of disturbed sand and gorse." He shook his head irritably. "He's not very forthcoming with information, isn't Howell."

"You certainly know your stuff, Murray. Trouble is, doesn't all this apply to Quint too?"

"No. They haven't found his dabs on the woman. Mind you, that's not necessarily conclusive. He could have worn gloves. Let's imagine he was hiding in the dunes and he saw the argument between Flick and Winnie, figured he might be in with a chance, when she rejected him, he reverted to plan A and knifed her, calmly leaving Flick's prints on her neck. Two birds and one sharp knife; dealt with the woman who rejected him, and dealt with the bloke who caused her to reject him."

Curnow frowned. "And gave me a class one headache at the same time." He glanced at his watch. "Pushing three o'clock. Time I wasn't here. Been nice rapping with you. Enjoy the show tonight."

They watched him leave the bar, and Owen commented,

"Ace guy. Really funny."

Joe scowled. "Yeah. In 1981."

George and Owen opted for a final drink, and Joe was not far behind Curnow leaving the bar, from where he made his way down to the harbour and looked over the assortment of cargo, private and pleasure craft, before ambling along the wall side towards the car park and the bus.

Crossing between the parked cars, he bumped into Eleanor.

She greeted him with a smile. "Oh, hello. Having a good day?"

"Not so you'd notice. How about you?" He nodded at her empty shopping bag.

She gave a small, embarrassed little laugh. "Hardly. I came looking for one or two bits and pieces, but couldn't find anything that took my fancy. Can I give you a lift back to Gittings?"

"I wouldn't give them the satisfaction." He checked his watch. "I'd better get back to the bus. I'll see you later."

"I hope so."

Satisfied with her last words, he left her, and made his way to the coach, where Keith already had the door open, and was waiting for the party to get back.

"You taking the jump seat again, Joe?"

"Yep. Brenda's not talking to me."

"So I hear. Have you made any progress on these thefts?"

"Nope. Not likely to either." Joe was aware that his tones were clipped, disinterested. He sighed. "You're a regular driver, Keith, and how many holidays and outings have you taken us on? Too many to count. And how many times have we had members complaining of bits and pieces stolen?"

Mort Norris and Mavis Barker arrived, and got on the bus while Keith appeared to give Joe's question some thought. "Almost never. The only trouble we've ever had is when you poked your nose into things that don't concern you."

"Yes, well, this time I kept my nose out, and I'm still in trouble."

George and Owen were amongst the stragglers, as a result

of which it was almost quarter past four before Keith began the return drive. As with the outbound journey, some people greeted Joe, others ignored him, and he ignored all of them, concentrating instead on a copy of *Dr No*, the next Bond novel after *From Russia With Love*, which he had bought at a charity shop at the top end of Market Jew Street and by the time they got back to Gittings, 007 was already facing an uncomfortable interview with M.

As they left the bus, most of the passengers headed back to their caravans, one or two made for the cafeteria, but Joe passed through the entertainment centre into the show bar, where he pulled Quint Ambrose to one end of the bar.

"You know they've arrested Flick?"

Quint's response was predictable. "Good. It's time someone walled him up."

"How much of the argument between him and Winnie did you see?"

It was a shot in the dark, but unexpectedly productive. Quint's colour drained, and he went immediately on the defensive. "I don't know what you mean."

"Your reaction tells me different. You were there, weren't you? You saw the fight between them. Did you see Flick stab her?"

His face fell. "No, I didn't. I'd already talked to her, told her how I felt, begged her to give me a chance, but she didn't wanna know. So I came away, and as I was walking back to the park, I saw Flick on the other path, walking towards her, so I hung around just to see what would happen."

Joe silently congratulated himself on his insight. "Go on."

"I tell you, she was all right when I left her. I didn't hurt her. But I could hear them arguing. Her more than Flick. I don't know what it was about, but she was threatening to blow the whistle. I couldn't hear what he was saying. Not properly. But then, all of a sudden, he grabbed her by the throat."

"And you didn't want to dash in like a knight in shining armour, rescuing your damsel in distress?" Joe's voice dripped cynical disbelief.

"No. She made it plain that she didn't want me, and I thought, sod it; if he batters her, she deserves it. So I turned and walked away."

Joe recreated the scene in his imagination. "Did she fight back?"

Quint nodded. "She was a tough cookie. You didn't start with her without expecting some comeback. But Tolley's way bigger than her. She never had a chance."

"How much attention were you really paying? Can you tell me which hand he grabbed her with?"

A puzzled frown and Quint's young face spoke for itself. "I never took no notice. What difference does it make?"

"A lot, trust me. Sixty years ago, Flick would have faced the noose for this kind of crime, and someone noticing something like that could have made the difference between life and death."

From the bar, Joe made his way to the bottom of the auditorium, where members of the entertainments staff were gathered around a single table.

"Hiya," he greeted them cheerily. "Listen, is there any danger I could talk to you for a few minutes?"

A young blonde, whose nametag announced her to be Dorinda, spoke for the rest of them. "If you're a variety agent, you're more than welcome."

"No. I'm a cook and I own my own café. I might be looking for kitchen staff."

A red haired young man, one of the dancers, laughed. "You're about as funny as Charlie."

"Talking of whom, where is he?"

"Sleeping it off," Dorinda said.

"Is he on split shifts this week, too? Like your boss, Eleanor?"

Dorinda's brow furrowed. "Eleanor's on split shifts every week. She prefers it that way." As quickly as she had made the announcement, she changed the subject. "What is it we can do for you, Mr Murray? Is it about Winnie?"

Joe nodded and pulled the seat to join them. "But for a couple of exceptions, I can't find anyone with a good word to say about her."

"You won't find anything different here, either," Dorinda assured him. "She was selfish, egotistical, over-ambitious, and had a voice like a foghorn."

Joe suppressed his irritation at the observation. "Professional jealousy?" he asked.

Dorinda laughed harshly. "She had nothing I needed to be jealous about, other than maybe the size of her bosom."

There was a general murmur of agreement around the table.

"Is there a hierarchy in place?" His question met with blank stares. "A pecking order? And was she at the top of it?"

Dorinda took a drink from a glass of what looked like lemonade and Joe remembered Winnie telling him that they were not allowed to drink when they were on duty (a rule that obviously did not apply to Charlie Curnow).

She put the glass down, and said, "Officially, there is no pecking order. We're all on the same, crap wages, and we answer to Charlie, but Winnie got it into her head that because she was the solo singer, that she was more important than us."

The others again agreed, and chipped in with examples, such as Winnie's refusal to help with the preparation of scenery, or her tantrums when their routines moved too fast for the tempo at which she was singing.

Joe realised he would learn little from these people, and he concluded, "None of you will be too worried about what happened to her, then?"

Dorinda again spoke up for them. "Nobody here would have hurt her. We're not like that... Well, Flick maybe, but the cops have arrested him, haven't they? The rest of us, we're mates, and we look out for each other. I'm sorry she's dead, but I have to say, I'm not sorry that she's no longer part of our team. Good riddance is what I say."

***

Brenda was busy in their shared caravan when Joe got back. Rather than face her, he climbed into his hired car, took out his smartphone and called Hattie O'Neill.

She sounded tired and irritable, and she could offer no news on those items stolen from 3rd Age Club members.

"I've no sympathy for them, Hattie," Joe replied. "Anyway, that's not what I'm ringing about. You have Flick Tolley's fingerprints on Winnie's neck. Which hand?"

"That's a strange kind of question, Joe. Does it matter?"

"Yes. In fact, I'd go so far as to say that it's vital."

"Hang on a minute, and I'll check."

There was a bump as she put the phone on the desk, and he could hear the clack and clatter of keys as she interrogated the computer. While he was waiting for her to come back to him, the caravan door opened, and Brenda marched past stiff-backed and ignoring him as she had done for most of the last thirty-six hours. He scowled after her, and was strongly tempted to let down the window and shout something, but he refrained. It would be childish, and anyway, Hattie was about to come back on the line.

"I've got it. His right hand. Now tell me what difference it makes."

"It might not prove him innocent, but I have a witness who saw the argument between them, and the witness insists that Flick was facing her when he grabbed her by the throat."

Hattie was silent for a moment. "If that's so, it would be difficult for him to stab her under her rib cage below the left breast."

"Yes, but not impossible. If he pushed her to the ground first, he could still have done it. Do you know whether she was standing or lying on her back when she was stabbed?"

"No. We don't. I can ask our pathologist for his opinion. Who is this witness, Joe? We need to speak to him."

"Quint Ambrose. Proper name is Quentin. He's a barman here at Gittings. I told you about him. He was besotted with Winnie, and to be honest, he has just as big a motive as Flick. Maybe bigger."

"We'll be out to speak to him tomorrow morning. Thanks for this, Joe. It's one I owe you."

"Remember that when I call the favour in."

Chapter Fifteen

"You're saying that Flick might be innocent?"

Eleanor was understandably concerned for the welfare (or otherwise) of one of her staff members, and while Joe again prepared toast for them, she had asked about the state of the investigation, deferring to his superior knowledge of police methods and his own investigative ability.

Joe felt quite flattered by it. Throughout Yorkshire in general, Sanford in particular, he was known as an astute observer, a man who missed nothing, moreover a man who could string arguments together to lead to a logical conclusion... even if that conclusion was wrong. But he wondered how much further Eleanor's interest went. Three nights in a row he had passed time in her bed, indulging their passion to a mutually satisfying conclusion, and when he considered that in conjunction with the excommunication many of his old friends had heaped upon him, he began to wonder whether his earlier conclusion was the right one. Maybe it was time to start afresh somewhere other than Yorkshire.

"I don't say it proves him innocent," he insisted, "but it does place a question mark over his guilt." He handed Eleanor a plate containing two slices of toast and butter, and helped himself to a second plate, before sitting at the table with her. "You see, Eleanor, when these things come to court, guilt and innocence don't always enter into the argument. It's all about the jury on the day, and the guidance the judge gives them in his summing up. Under the law, if there is reasonable doubt, then a man cannot be found guilty, but 'reasonable doubt' has never been defined. I could stand up in court as a witness, and say that Flick could not possibly have murdered her, but if the prosecution have evidence that she was thrown to the ground first, then the jury would have to weigh that against my evidence, or rather, Quint's evidence."

She swallowed a mouthful of toast. "You're very passionate about this, aren't you, Joe?"

"With good reason," he replied, and went on to detail the two cases in which he had been charged with murder. "It's a terrible crime," he concluded. "No one has the right to take another's life, and I've always held the view that anyone who does, should forfeit his or her life, but in a prison cell and not necessarily at the end of a rope. By the same token, the system is supposed to ensure that no innocent man or woman should spend time in prison."

"It goes wrong, though, doesn't it?"

"More so these days than in the past, or so it seems."

He was about to press her and the possibility of moving from Yorkshire to Cornwall when she forestalled the question. "So, did you find anything worthwhile in Penzance?"

"Pretty boring to be honest. No different to Sanford or Leeds. How about you? Were you looking for anything special?"

"I was thinking of treating myself to a new iPad or something similar, but the prices are outrageous."

"Tell me about. I was looking in that second hand shop on Market Jew Street, but even they—"

The caravan door burst open, cutting Joe off, and Charlie Curnow stepped in.

He reeled drunkenly, stared around, concentrated on them, and with a hiccup, laughed. "Oops. Sorry, Ellie. Wrong caravan. 'Night, luv, 'night, Murray." He staggered out again.

Eleanor clucked impatiently. "Plastered. Again."

"So much for discretion." Joe was in a hurry to finish his tea and toast. "Does that happen often?"

"A few times every season. When he's seriously drunk. And thank God he is smashed out of his brains." She chuckled gleefully. "Don't worry, Joe, by tomorrow morning, he'll have forgotten that you were here."

"I wasn't thinking of me. My reputation's in the gutter right now, so I don't care what anyone thinks or says about me, but you have a position to maintain." He checked his watch and read midnight. "I'd better get moving. Tomorrow night? Or would you like to cry off?"

"Let's play it by ear, eh?"

Joe stepped out into the chilly night, and made his way along the lines to his caravan, which (mercifully) was in complete darkness. When he let himself in, he soon learned that he was alone. Not that he was afraid of a confrontation with Brenda, but things would likely be said which he (or she) would later regret.

He spent half an hour bringing his notes up-to-date, during which he once again recalled he had seen Eleanor in Penzance, which reminded him (as if he needed it) of his 'exercises' with her earlier, and his appointment with her tomorrow evening. Just before one in the morning, he took to his bed, but as before, sleep only came with difficulty. His mind turned and whirled with developing events, the problem of Wynette Kalinowski's murder compounding with the trouble between him and the people he had always considered his friends, and it seemed to him that he was living through a nightmare, and he was at the mercy of events, able to do nothing but wait to wake up.

***

When he climbed out of bed a little before eight in the morning, the sun was shining once again. The bus was scheduled to leave for Tintagel at nine, and Keith had assured them that it would take about an hour and a half to get there.

Over a bowl of cereal and a cup of strong coffee, he considered the prospect of ninety minutes on a bus full of people, most of whom would ignore him, and decided he did not want it. He rang Alec Staines, and told him, "I'll make my way there in the hire car, and catch up with some of you in Tintagel. Let Keith know, will you? It'll save him waiting for me."

Alec agreed, and at ten o'clock, Joe, wrapped in his fleece against a cold wind, climbed into his rental, fired the engine, and set off after them.

He was pleased to find that the A30 running north from Hayle was a broad, high-speed, dual carriageway, and the same could be said of the A39 when he came off near Columb St Major, but a mile further on, when it turned north for Tintagel, it was reduced to a single carriageway, and despite its official classification as a trunk road, it was, like the road from Penzance to Land's End, often narrow and awkward to negotiate. Overtaking a tractor pulling a large trailer loaded with bales of hay was a work of art, and to Joe it felt like he had followed it for miles, even though it was actually less than five hundred yards.

One and a quarter hours after leaving Gittings, he finally pulled into Tintagel village, slotted the car into a free space on the pay-and-display car park, climbed out and breathed in the fresh, ocean air. After the confines of the little car, it seemed fresher than that in Hayle. A trick of the mind, he diagnosed. The air in Hayle was festering, but that had more to do with human nature than meteorology.

The day would not be much more exciting than Wednesday in Penzance. Tintagel had little to offer other than souvenir shops, and some spectacular views from the cliff tops. He took photographs of the Old Post Office, which allegedly dated back to the fourteenth century, and the more recent King Arthur's Hall, and in one shop he found CDs of instrumental folk music from the south-western peninsula. After listening to samples from some tracks, Joe decided that they were worth the better part of £20, and bought them.

He had lunch with the Staineses in one of the many little teashops, but he flatly refused to accompany them on the walk down to the Beach Café and the subsequent climb up to the ruins of the castle. Instead, when they left him, he bought a visitor's guide book and several postcards.

By two o'clock he was seriously losing interest, and he returned to his car for the journey back to Hayle.

Keith was already standing by the bus, waiting for the

passengers to return, and as Joe got to his car, Sylvia Goodson detached herself from the little clutch of people which included Tanner, Dalmer and Brenda, and came to speak with him.

"Don't you think this ridiculous farce has gone on long enough, Joe?" she asked.

"I didn't start it. Les did, and Brenda supported him, and so did other people."

"They were looking for you to help, Joe."

"No. They were looking for someone to slag off the management at Gittings, when in fact, the problem was theirs. They were warned about the thefts on that site."

Sylvia took his hand. "Please, Joe. You are one of the stalwarts of this club. We don't want to lose you."

He modulated his anger. "You're very kind, Sylvia. You always have been. But you should be telling Les that, not me."

And with that, he climbed behind the wheel of his hired car, started the engine and set off on the return journey. Although she had only the best of intentions, Sylvia had inadvertently triggered the anger in him again, and the further he was from them, the better he felt.

Six miles from Tintagel, he picked up the A39 south of Camelford, turned right, settled his speed at a conservative fifty, and then checked the time on the dashboard. It was too early to go back to Gittings, and he tossed the idea of Newquay or Perranporth around his head. He had almost decided on the latter when his phone rang. Ever cautious, he pulled into a layby, picked up the instrument and checked the menu. Hattie.

He applied the handbrake, and made the connection.

"Afternoon, lass, what can I do you for?"

"Just touching base, really, Joe. We're still questioning Flick and Quint, and both of them are denying any part in Wynette's murder. I wondered if you had anything for us?"

"No. Sorry. Have you had the full post mortem results?"

"Funny you should mention that. I'm at the hospital in Truro now. I'm with Wynette's mother. She's given us formal identification, and obviously, she's very upset."

A surge of interest shot through Joe. "Tell you what, Hattie, can you get her to wait until I get there? I'd like a word with her."

"Well, I can ask her. Where are you now?"

"On the A39, a few miles south of Camelford."

"It'll take you about three quarters of an hour to get here. Just program your satnav for the hospital in Truro. I'll meet you either outside or in the cafeteria there."

Joe killed the call, carried out Hattie's instructions and programmed Truro hospital in to his satnav, then started the engine, and set off.

As he was so fond of saying, the best witness in any crime was always the victim, and that held true even in a case of murder where the victim could no longer speak for him, or her, self. He had spent the last five days on the periphery of this appalling crime, and had learned very little of the woman herself. That was largely thanks to Howell's surly and uncooperative approach. In the past, he had always delved into the victim and the suspects from the off, but the inspector's recalcitrance coupled to Joe's problems with the 3rd Age Club had seen him make little headway. Sure, he'd spoken to Flick, sure he'd spoken to Quint, Curnow, Eleanor, and even Winnie's fellow performers, but none of them confessed to knowing too much about her, and with the exception of Eleanor and possibly Quint, each had painted a derogatory picture of her. What he needed now was the other side of the coin, even if her mother's opinion was rose coloured.

The hospital was easy enough to find, opposite an industrial estate on the road leading into Truro. Finding a parking spot was a different proposition, and when Joe finally managed to grab a space, he was stunned by the cost. Putting aside his natural niggardliness, he paid the fee and made his way towards the entrance, where he found Hattie perched on a bench with Janet Kalinowski, Wynette's mother.

Hattie introduced them, Joe shook hands and sat alongside her.

"Allow me to offer my condolences, Mrs Kalinowski," he said. "I don't know how much Hattie's told you, but I'm a private investigator from the North of England, and I'm down here on holiday. I ended up involved in this business purely by accident, and I'd like to ask you about Wynette."

Aged somewhere in her fifties, she was withered and drawn, pale-faced, and played constantly with a handkerchief, knotting and twisting it between her agitated fingers.

"I already told the police everything," she said. "And I don't care what everyone says, my Winnie was a good girl. She had the voice of an angel, and when she told me she wanted to be a singer, it was the proudest moment of my life. And she shouldn't have been wasting her time on that holiday camp. She was better than that. She could have been a star, she could."

Having heard the girl sing on Saturday night, Joe reserved his opinion, which was completely the opposite of Janet's.

"You say you don't care what everyone says? What were they saying?"

"They said she was a…" Janet struggle to get the words out. "A tramp."

She burst into tears, and Hattie made an effort to calm her. Joe felt guilty. Women who cried always did that to him.

Eventually, Janet gained some control over her emotions, and went on. "She was always short of money, but when she went to Gittings, she was suddenly flush. Well, I know they don't pay that much in wages, and for a little while I thought she was… you know…"

Janet trailed off again, and Joe was left to fill in the blanks. It was obvious that the woman thought her daughter was prostituting herself.

"I get the picture," he replied. "Did she tell you how she really came by the money?"

Janet nodded tearfully. "I don't like to say, cos she's no longer here to defend herself, but she told me she was working with other people and they were stealing from the campers and selling the stuff on. I don't mind telling you, Mr

Murray, I played the merry hell with her, and she was sorry. Crying, she was. Well, she was brought up properly, see. She was always taught never to steal from anyone."

Joe was hesitant asking the next question. "You didn't threaten to drag her along to the police station?"

He expected more tears, but Janet remained strong. "You're a foreigner in these parts, so maybe they do it different where you come from, but you never sell your own down the river."

He did not get into the debate. The threat to take a son or daughter to the law was often enough to change behaviour in his world, and he could never recall any parent actually carrying it through.

Janet's composure began to weaken again. "I could see she really was sorry, but she told me that it was the only chance she had of breaking into the big time. She needed the money. Once she had enough, she could go to London and audition for television shows like *Big Talent* and *The Singer Not the Song*." Tears welled in her eyes again and a more wistful note sounded in her voice. "She would have paid it back. Every penny. I know she would."

On the admission that Wynette was involved in organised thefts from the caravans, Joe cast a meaningful glance at Hattie, who shrugged with her eyes. Joe guessed that whatever Janet was telling him now, she had already told Hattie, and that would give the police another angle on the interrogation of Flick and Quint.

And as he wound the conversation down, with trite and inconsequential platitudes, the several, disparate strands of these crimes began to coalesce in his head. What price Wynette had threatened to expose the people at the core of this ring of thieves? And if so, had they decided that it was safest to shine her on? And if his assumptions were anything like true, what were the odds on the involvement of Tolley and/or Ambrose. It would, he reasoned, be one or the other, not both. The way they had been fighting in St Ives precluded that.

Joe began to run the logic circuits of his mind as Hattie

arranged for a patrol car to take Janet home, by the time the sergeant returned to sit with him, he had come to some early and speculative conclusions.

"Concentrate on Ambrose," he advised her.

"How come?"

"He accused Tolley of drug dealing. Now let's imagine that one or both of them was involved in this organised theft. It can't be both, or Ambrose wouldn't have accused Tolley of anything, and if he did, Tolley would have countered the accusation by claiming that it was Ambrose dealing drugs. You follow me so far?"

Hattie nodded. "It makes a sort of sense."

"Ambrose accusing Tolley, and Flick's dabs on Winnie's neck was a perfect diversion. It draws your investigation away from potential involvement in organised crime, and focuses on the one man."

"So how come Flick didn't accuse Quint of running this gang of thieves?"

"Tough question to answer, and I can only guess, but I think Flick is hedging his bets. What are the chances of charging and convicting him?"

"Put it this way, I've got a better chance of winning the lottery this weekend."

"So when you let him go, and you release Quint for lack of evidence, Flick is in the perfect position to put pressure on Quint. Make sure a few quid comes his way, and he'll keep his mouth shut about the stealing."

Hattie chewed her lip. "What we really need is to pin down the man or woman at the heart of this organised theft, isn't it?"

"Yes. And what price that could be Quint Ambrose? Aside from working behind the bar at Gittings, what do you know about him?"

"Local yokel, like me. Comes from Helston originally. A few cautions for the usual teenage stuff: nuisance, affray, fighting, drunk and disorderly. You know what I mean. Worked in the licensed trade virtually since he was eighteen years old. Apart from that, as far as we can see, there's nothing else to know." Hattie went on with more enthusiasm. "Flick is a different matter. He's been a bad bugger most of his adult life. He served eighteen months in a young offenders' unit. Taking and driving away. While he was in there, he took a course in drama, song and dance, and when he came out, he started to get proper work, and ever since then, he's been clean, but he does have a reputation as a hard case."

Joe chuckled. "My nephew was a forward for the Sanford Balls, rugby league team, and you wouldn't fancy arguing with him, but the truth is, he's as soft as freshly baked bread… only not as appetising." He frowned. "I was talking to Eleanor Dorning the other… day." Joe almost slipped and said 'night'. "She assured me that Gittings run criminal record checks on all employees, and they came in clean. Charlie Curnow told me the same thing."

Hattie was not surprised. "Spent conviction, Joe. It is over five years ago, and unless they did a real, in-depth search, they never turn it up." She got to her feet. "I'd better get back to the station. Looks like we'll be at it most of the night with these two. I'll catch you later."

Chapter Sixteen

From the hospital to Gittings was a journey of about twenty miles, and would take less than half an hour, but it was a time during which matters began to coalesce in Joe's mind.

The two issues which had plagued him for the last few days were all part of one problem, and he was now convinced that Wynette had been murdered after she threatened to expose the ringleaders of this organised gang.

When he rejoined the A30, six miles west of Truro, it also became clear to him that although Flick or Quint must have killed her, neither of them was likely to be the prime receiver of stolen goods. In order to sell the swag on, the 'fence' had to have buyers, as they would need to be spread across the county. Both men (in Joe's opinion) were too young to have set up such a network, and that naturally shifted his focus to Charlie Curnow.

By his own admission, the camp comedian had been what Liverpudlians would describe as a 'scally' all his life. A dishonourable discharge from an esteemed regiment such as the Royal Marines for bootlegging, and an admission that he regularly took delivery of contraband here in Cornwall, spoke of a man who was strapped for cash, and had little respect for the law, moreover, a man who was willing to take risks no matter how slight. Would he stop at murder? He may not be ready to carry it out himself, but faced with the real danger of a long prison sentence, he would probably not hesitate to put someone else up to it, and that brought Flick back into the equation.

It was a delicately balanced situation. Joe had to be certain that he had it right. Accuse the wrong man, and he would put the alternative suspects on alert.

Coming off the A30 at the Loggan's roundabout, and dropping onto the narrow lanes which would lead him to the park, he cursed Inspector Howell. Hattie had kept him up to speed, been glad of his assistance, but Howell was more reluctant with information, and if Joe knew anything about the police, the inspector would know an awful lot more than his sergeant.

Going through the park gates, he noticed Keith wandering round his bus, checking it over. A matter of routine for their driver. Joe stopped and called to him.

"Where is everyone?"

"Coventry," Keith replied with a grin. "Oops, sorry, you're the one in Coventry. That's where they've sent you."

"Their choice and their loss." Joe eyed the bus. "What are you doing?"

"Well, in case you've forgotten, we're all going home in less than thirty-six hours, and I have to make sure the bus is ready. I'll be taking it to the nearest filling station tomorrow, to fuel up, then taking the rest of the day off before I drive you pains in the backside home."

Joe put the car into gear. "That's what we love about you, Keith. Your charity."

He knocked the handbrake off, and continued driving along the caravan lines, eventually reversing into the slot outside his van.

The time was a little after five o'clock, and already the day was on the wane, the sun dipping towards the western horizon. He was not surprised to find himself alone again, especially after what Keith had just told him. He made himself a cup of tea, laid out a change of clothes, and began to pack away the things he would no longer need, ready for the journey home. And throughout, he recognised his actions as those of a man in need of something to do, something to occupy his mind while it turned the two problems over and over.

The attitude of his friends was beginning to get to him, and he began to doubt whether the term 'friends' was still accurate. At the same time, he recognised in himself a distancing from everything around him, which could be tracked back to the death of Denise Latham, killed by the same crazed individual who had pursued him in Palmanova and then in Sanford when he returned.

But the reaction of the 3rd Age Club annoyed him more. Was he not entitled to a life of his own? Where were they when he needed support after Denise's death?

And with a sudden clarity of insight, he realised that there was an element missing. Sheila. Of the inseparable trio which comprised her, Brenda and him, she was the strongest. She could be snappy and outspoken, but almost without exception, she would bring an element of level-headed sanity, derived from an acute intelligence and understanding of human nature, to any situation. Her late husband, Peter, had been an inspector in the Sanford police, and Sheila had worked for many years as secretary at Sanford Comprehensive School, a position in which she had to contend with the tantrums of teenage pupils and adult staff alike.

Her marriage, announced during the treasure hunt in Whitby, had signalled the first splinter in the triumvirate at the head of the Sanford 3rd Age Club, but neither he nor Brenda had considered its effect on their half-century friendship.

After taking a shower and shaving, he hooked up his laptop, went online, and called her through Skype.

It was not Sheila who answered, but Martin, her new husband.

"I'm sorry, Joe, but she's really ill." Martin's unshaven features were grim, concerned. "Boa Vista was a bad choice as it turned out."

"And what's the problem?" Joe demanded. "New Delhi belly?"

"Certainly enteritis. The local doctor's taken a look at her, but it's not good. We're due home on Saturday, and I'll get her to the nearest doctor or hospital the minute we get back. Can I help at all?"

Joe shrugged into the webcam. "It's this business between me and the rest of the club. Most of them are not talking to me. They think I've deserted them." He sighed. "We've had spats before, but never anything this serious, and to be honest, Martin, I'm getting more than a little peed off with it."

"Sheila's told me some of it. I'm a teacher, remember, and the only advice I can give youngsters when they come to me with this kind of trouble, is walk away. You're a grown man, Joe. You know your own mind, and if you prefer the company of this woman, then it's your decision. Your life. You're not answerable to anyone for it. I don't know if that helps."

"It might. You're not saying anything I hadn't already thought of. Thanks, Martin. Give Sheila my regards. I hope she's feeling better soon."

Joe killed the connection, and stared into space. The brief conversation with Martin had got him nowhere. Keith pointed out that there were just thirty-six hours between now and the long trek home. Thirty-six hours during which, like it or not, he would have to make some firm decisions.

He was still contemplating the issue when Brenda stepped through the caravan door, ignored him completely, and went straight to her bedroom.

Friends, not friends, it didn't matter. He had to tell her about Sheila.

Almost an hour passed before she emerged from the shower and her bedroom, dressed for the evening, and she was preparing to walk out of the van, when he stopped her.

"Sheila is very ill."

She turned to face him. "You called her?" Her tone of voice made it sound as if he had committed some unforgivable sin.

"I tried to, but she's too sick. I spoke to Martin instead. Enteritis. I thought you should know."

Her anger began to rise. "What you mean is you were looking for sympathy."

Joe matched her ire with some of his own. "Don't talk so bloody soft. When the hell have I ever needed sympathy? And if you think I give a hoot about those silly sods sending me to Coventry, you've another think coming. You can take your opinions and stick them where the sun don't shine."

About to leave again, Brenda whirled on him. Her face was ablaze, her eyes pinpoint darts, aimed at his furious features. "You are an absolute disgrace. You've abandoned your friends, people you've known for half a century, for the sake of some woman you've been jumping all week."

"I've done nothing of the kind. If those alleged friends hadn't been so stupid, they would not have left anything of value lying around their caravans for the thieves to take, and for your information, I have more on my mind than Eleanor Dorning. I always have, and this holiday is no different."

"Nothing is ever different with you, is it? You're poking your nose into another killing that doesn't concern you, but this time it's not just the police you're annoying, it's your friends, who you're ignoring, even though they're victims too." Anger finally got the better of her. "I've had it with you. I never want to see or speak to you again. And you can take this as my notice. I quit The Lazy Luncheonette."

Joe responded half-heartedly. "You can't quit. You're a part owner."

"Then I'll sell my share back to you."

"You can't. You never bought it in the first place. It was a gift."

"Then take it back. I don't want it. I don't want you. I don't want anything to do with you. Ever."

Joe zipped up his fleece. "Suit yourself."

He pushed past her, stormed from the caravan, slammed the door behind him, and Brenda flopped onto the settee. Tears welled in her eyes. It was too much to take in. Fifty years of friendship shattered in the space of four days, and all thanks to a woman who couldn't keep her knickers on.

The thought gave rise to her own reputation for being too free and easy. It was not true, but it was a common misconception. Her friends, however, knew different. Sure, she dated different men, but ninety-nine percent of those dates went no further than a goodnight kiss. The number of 'lovers' (her mind automatically placed the word in speech marks) was few. George Robson and Stewart Dalmer. And of course, there was Joe. A brief fling with him in Weston-super-Mare had been enjoyable, but destined to go nowhere, and they had allowed it to peter out naturally. Dalmer had only been added this week, and only then because of Joe's behaviour both here and in Whitby during the summer.

Sitting there, determined not to cry, she felt as if her whole life was crumbling around her. She needed Sheila, but Sheila was four thousand miles away, acclimatising herself to her new life, her new husband.

Following Joe's lead, she powered up her laptop, and called Sheila. Martin answered and told her the same as he had told Joe, but while he was talking to her, Sheila appeared. She looked pale and haggard, and not as serene as she had been earlier in the week.

"I heard you talking to Martin, I thought I'd better catch up with you now. We're due out of Cape Verde on Saturday afternoon, and we'll be spending most of tomorrow getting ready, and you'll be on the bus home longer than we'll be on the plane. I'm very unwell, and I plan to rest as much as I can between now and Saturday, so I may not get the chance to speak to you again."

Brenda's natural concern for Sheila was overridden by her secret relief at being able to talk to her, and it did not take long for Sheila to realise that there was something so much more amiss than Brenda had told her over the last few days. In the space of the next twenty minutes, Brenda poured out the entire tale.

It was one of those curious anomalies that Sheila had always been the one capable of the most cutting remarks, but her occasional acid candour was held in check by an astute intelligence and an innate ability to stand outside an argument and observe.

Her response to Brenda's story was typical. "Quite honestly, you both need your bottoms smacking." Having made her position clear, she took a more conciliatory approach. "You have to make allowances for him. He's been drifting ever since Denise's death, and that business in Palmanova frightened him."

"Sheila, he came down on the side of this awful place, rather than backing his friends."

"That's not strictly true, is it? At least, not the way you've been telling me, it isn't. It doesn't matter where you are, what kind of holiday you choose, you are responsible for your own personal effects, not the hotel or park owners, and if the members have been warned of persistent thefts, then they should have taken appropriate steps and not left valuables lying around their caravans."

"They hadn't been warned," Brenda insisted. "Joe never bothered to tell anyone."

"I was just coming to that because it's symptomatic of Joe's recent self-centredness. How long have we known him? Fifty years? Longer? He's grumpy and outspoken, but he's never put himself first. Unlike Les, who wants to run the club, Joe was a servant. He's lost sight of that, and he needs reminding of it."

"I have reminded him."

"Yes. But a little too forcefully. He needs encouraging to come back onside, Brenda, and the way you went about it won't work. He'll respond in the way he handles the police. Out and out obduracy. Pig-headed stubbornness."

The sense of Sheila's argument began to sink in. "Then what am I going to do?"

"Keep your distance for the time being. That probably won't be an issue, because he'll keep away from you. Then choose your moment, and talk to him, and I mean talk, not rant."

Brenda agreed and after a further ten minutes of general chat, during which they discussed Sheila's illness, and Sheila made an effort (not entirely successful) to show Brenda some of the photographs she had taken of the island, they closed the call, and Brenda shut down her laptop.

An hour later, with the time coming up to 8 o'clock, the September/October night had already closed in. She put on her coat, and left the caravan for the short walk to the entertainment centre.

She was ambling past the next van when Sylvia and

Tanner stepped out, and she waited until they fell in alongside her. As they walked along, she told them of the argument with Joe, and her discussion with Sheila.

Tanner was uncharacteristically diffident. "I suppose she has a point, and I must confess, I think I may have been a little too hasty in calling the vote." He cleared his throat. "I may have to eat humble pie."

"I don't know," Brenda said. "He was in a hell of a mood when he stormed out, and his comments on the club were not complimentary." She sighed into the night. "What are we going to do?"

Tanner sucked in his breath. "I already know what to do. I'm resigning the Chair."

Brenda stopped in her tracks. Was this just a night for shocks? "For heaven's sake why?"

"I'm guilty as charged," Sylvia said. "I talked him into it, Brenda. You know my feelings for Les. He's a good man, but his management style is not consistent with the running of a social club. It's better if someone else takes over."

"And your man has already expressed an interest," Tanner said.

Brenda frowned. "My man?"

"Dalmer," Les confirmed. "Like Murray, he runs his own business, so he's perfectly accustomed to decision-making. Unlike Murray, he's efficient. Do I need to say any more?"

There was something in Tanner's tone which indicated a subtext, but Brenda could not get a handle on it.

"You don't approve?"

"As the outgoing Chair, Brenda, it's hardly for me to say, but privately, I don't think Stewart is the man for the job."

As they neared the entertainment complex, and headed into the cafeteria, Brenda began to wish that she could wave some kind of magic wand and put everything back as it was in the past. She remembered entertaining the same feelings when her husband passed away. But there was no such thing as a magic wand, and the only way back was through hard work, and even then there were no guarantees of recovering former glories.

Chapter Seventeen

Joe stomped away from the caravan with the intention of going to the show bar cafeteria for his evening meal, but he had gone less than five yards when he changed his mind, turned back and climbed into his hired Citroen. Firing the engine, he gunned the accelerator and ignoring the speed limits and speed humps, tore out of the park, picked up the main road and headed for the Smugglers Inn on the road to Penzance.

Eleanor did not finish her shift until eight o'clock, and that was fine with him. Later in the evening, when he had calmed down, he would want her company, but right now all he wanted was to be alone, let the seething rage settle.

And as he put distance between himself and Gittings, he began to calm down, and with that came clarity of thought.

He didn't care whether Brenda was right or wrong. It was his life to lead as he saw fit, and if that excluded the Sanford 3rd Age Club, then so be it.

Twenty minutes later, settling into a booth, ordering a well done steak and a glass of lager, he took out his smartphone and called his nephew, Lee.

"All right, Uncle Joe? Are you having a good time?"

"I'm doing all right, lad," he lied. "Just ringing to check whether there's been any problems while I've been away."

"No." Lee sounded defensive. "I can manage, you know. I mean, I've been working there long enough to know what to do."

Joe smiled to himself at the manner in which Lee had misunderstood his initial query. "I know you have, and I wasn't doubting you."

"Good. It's been as busy as it always is, and the brewery

men keep asking when you're due back." Lee laughed. "I think they miss the way you insult them."

Joe did not find the comment funny, and once he had asked after Cheryl and young Danny, and received assurances that everyone was fine, he ended the call. If anything, it had reinforced an inkling that had been at the back of his mind since his return from Majorca via Tenerife and Cragshaven.

For one crazy moment, he considered calling back at the caravan, packing his bags and driving the hire car home, rather than waiting for the bus on Saturday morning. The rental agency was part of a nationwide group, and he could leave the car at the nearest branch to Sanford.

Common sense born of sheer bloody mindedness prevailed. Why should he? He paid his dues, paid for his week in Cornwall, so why should he turn and run away just because the rest of the membership (or that part of it which was in Hayle and had voted against him) was disenchanted with him? They would be glad to see the back of him, and he refused to give them the satisfaction of seeing him run.

But the thought gave rise to others, most of them centred on the appalling loneliness of his current situation. If he disappeared without trace, no one, other than a few individuals such as Lee, Cheryl, perhaps Gemma, would bat an eyelid. And the tiny notion which had been at the back of his mind a few moments ago, took on greater significance.

"The Lazy Luncheonette doesn't need me," he confessed to Eleanor when he joined her in her caravan two hours later. "And neither does the Sanford 3rd Age Club."

He took no pleasure in the announcement. He had given all his life to the café, and a sizeable proportion of the last seven or eight years to the 3rd Age Club, and the thought of putting them into the background was difficult.

By the same token, he was not the only man or woman in the world to turn their back on a previous life and start afresh even at his advancing age. Hadn't Alison done it when they divorced and she left for Tenerife? Like him, she was a Sanfordian through and through, but after splitting with Joe, she decided that the Canary Islands were preferable to West

Yorkshire, and she had never regretted the decision. Indeed, she had tried to persuade him to stay there when he fled to her after the events of Palmanova.

Eleanor was sympathetic. "Are you sure Brenda wasn't just sounding off?"

Joe shook his head and swilled brandy around a balloon. "I've known her since we were kids. We were at school together. I know the difference between meaning it and just getting her hair off. She meant it." He downed the brandy in one gulp. "Listen, I know people see me as an experienced short order cook, but there's more to me than that. I served my time in catering college. I can create the fancy meals people prefer these days, and I know how to pull a pint. Be honest with me, Eleanor, if I sold up, passed my share of the business to Lee, and moved down here, what would be my chances?"

She chewed her lip. "That's difficult to assess, Joe. You just said that you've given your life to your café. If you came down here, even if you could find premises, get permission, set them up, you still have to establish a reputation, and speaking frankly, Cornishmen are just as cliquey as Yorkshireman. It takes time to become accepted. On top of that, we don't get many truckers coming this far south. You'd be reliant on locals and the tourist trade, and as I say, the locals would take time to accept you, which means that between the end of September the beginning of April, you'd have a lean time."

For a moment, it occurred to Joe that she was trying to put him off, but with the perspicacity which led him to the conclusion that Sanford was a part of the past he needed to be without, he realised that she was merely cautioning him; advising him of the difficulties which would confront him.

With the promise that he would think seriously about it, they took to her bed, where they enjoyed each other for the second last time, and Joe sneaked from her caravan a little after midnight, and made his way to the accommodation he shared with Brenda.

It was rare that Joe got drunk. His hours of work had long

ago dissuaded him from an excess of alcohol. It was bad enough crawling out of bed in the middle of the night, without compounding matters with a storming hangover.

And for once, his sobriety saved him from serious injury. As he ambled along the gravel lane towards his caravan, a blaze of headlights came from behind, accompanied by the roar of an overstressed engine. Joe glanced over his shoulder, and saw the car bearing down on him at high speed. He threw himself to the right, landed on the grass and rolled over a couple of times, before sitting up and glaring at the retreating vehicle.

There was no mistaking the silver-grey Renault Clio. The shabby, peeling paintwork on the passenger door, the missing wheel trim from the front rim told him all he needed to know. Charlie Curnow. Drunk as a skunk again.

The caravan lights were out when he got there, and that was fine by him. Ten to one, Brenda was sleeping with Dalmer. He let himself in, cleaned himself up after rolling over the grass, made a cup of tea, and went to bed, killing all the lights before settling down for the night.

He was still awake an hour later when he heard Brenda come in, and he guessed she was alone. He could hear only her footsteps moving around the van, and there was no conversation. He guessed that the row would have put a damper on her ardour, and it was with more than a touch of schadenfreude that the idea pleased him. It served her right.

For one mad moment, he considered getting out of bed and confronting her, but he changed his mind. She would learn of any decision soon enough, even if that meant when they got back to Sanford.

Once again, sleep came only with difficulty. The events of the day, the argument earlier in the evening, his solitary meal followed by his debate with Eleanor and the subsequent excitement, preyed upon his mind.

In an effort to combat his disturbed thoughts, he turned his attention to the murder of Wynette Kalinowski. He had twenty-four hours in which to prove Flick Tolley and Quentin Ambrose innocent… or guilty, as the case may be.

But still sleep would not come. This time, however, it was something he was certain he had seen or heard over the last day or two, a tiny, insignificant detail, but one which his jackrabbit mind could not pin down.

Eventually, he drifted off to sleep, but he was up again just after half past six, and still the events of the previous day, the missing item in a murder enquiry, filled his mind.

He heard Brenda moving around in her room at eight o'clock, and determined to avoid her, he left the caravan, climbed into the rented car, and drove off. He didn't know where he was going, other than as far away from her and the other members of the 3rd Age Club as possible.

***

He took breakfast in a café on Market Jew Street in Penzance, the same one he had used a couple of days before, and as he ate, he wondered again about the etymology of the street's name. It seemed to him to have racist overtones, although he was probably way off the mark. He was surprised and amused to learn (after checking it out on the web via his smartphone) that the name was actually a corruption of *Marghas Yow*, a term from the original Cornish language which translated as nothing more sinister than *Thursday Market*, but it struck a chord with him. Back home in Sanford, Pitted Street generated mental images of a street full of potholes, but in fact it was a corruption of Pit Head Street.

It was another bright, sparkling and sunny morning, chilly out of the sun, but otherwise pleasant and mild, which was more than could be said for his mood. He was glad to be away from Gittings, even more so to be away from Brenda and the problems surrounding the people and the place, but those same issues still haunted him.

What chance would he and Eleanor have of a life together? He had not put the proposition to her, and even as he thought of it, the absurdity struck him. He had known the woman less than a week, and he had no idea whether she was interested in a long-term relationship. He was looking at the situation purely from his point of view, not hers. Had she not told him that first night she had never been in a serious relationship? And he knew little about her other than she was an excellent, vibrant and vigorous sexual partner; entirely the wrong basis for any kind of future.

Thinking of her reminded him of the way he had bumped into her on the car park two days previously. It was a damn shame. How could he persuade her to change her mind? Did he want to persuade her? Would he readily change his mind?

He was still musing on the matter when his gaze fell on the window display of Entiex across the street. His curiosity getting the better of him, when he finished his meal, he crossed the street and studied the range of smartphones, tablets and handheld video consoles, all of them second-hand, and all of them still comparatively expensive.

He was particularly taken with the various iPads and similar on offer. Wherever he went he carried his laptop, and it was cumbersome, especially when he was travelling abroad with the miserly weight restrictions airlines insisted upon.

On an impulse, he stepped into the shop. Ten o'clock in the morning, and it was not busy. There were one or two customers, browsers mainly, one engaging an assistant in conversation at the counter. The client was asking about a particular DSLR camera, and it called to mind Tanner's missing equipment. It would serve the silly sod right if his thousand pounds worth of camera turned up in a place like this.

With the customer at the counter at the forefront of his mind, he ambled along the displays of photographic equipment, and his blood ran cold.

There, at eye level, was a Canon EOS 250D, the same make and model Les Tanner had lost. What's more, the placard alongside it insisted that it came with two lenses, and a sturdy, photographer's shoulder bag, with compartments for the various other accoutrements. The particular instrument was expensive and there was nothing to suggest that it belonged to Tanner, but Joe did not trust coincidences. Too often, they turned out be anything but.

He marched up to the counter. "The Canon 250 in the case." He gestured at the locked display.

"Yes, sir, if you could give me a minute. I'm serving this gentleman."

"It's stolen."

Joe was aware of the amount of trouble his announcement could cause, especially if it turned out that he was wrong, but his words had the necessary effect. The assistant turned fiery eyes on him, and ran a hand through his scrub beard. "I beg your pardon?"

"You heard me."

"You're from the police, are you? Only you look a little short to be a cop. So what business is it of yours?"

"I'm making it my business because I think it belonged to a friend of mine, and it was stolen from his caravan three days ago."

The customer looked alarmed and beat a hasty retreat, but the assistant remained unimpressed. "We had proof of ownership. We always ask for proof of ownership."

"And the lady's name?"

The assistant did not pause to ask how Joe knew a woman had sold the camera to him. He called up the computer records, and at length, turned the laptop to face Joe.

"Linda Trelawney."

A second coincidence; the initials LT. Les Tanner? "Let's have a look at it before I call the cops."

"Now look—"

Joe took out his smartphone. "Either let me see it or I'll bell my very good friend, Detective Sergeant Harriet O'Neill, of the Devon and Cornwall Constabulary. I think she'll be interested."

Backed into a corner from which there was no escape, the assistant tromped along behind the displays, unlocked the appropriate cupboard, and took out the camera and its case. Returning to Joe, he planted the whole lot on the counter.

Joe ignored the camera body and lenses inside the bag, and instead checked the lid, where the metal identity tag was engraved *L.T.* That was enough for him.

"Okay, pal, here's the position. I believe this camera is the property of Leslie Tanner, of Sanford, West Yorkshire. It was stolen three days ago from his caravan on Gittings Holiday Park, in Hayle. And even if it wasn't, I have enough grounds for calling the police, and getting them to check the serial number. While they're doing that, I'll call Mr Tanner, and I'll get the number of his camera from him. If the two match, you are deep in the doggy-doo." Joe rang Hattie. A minute later, he came off the phone, and smiled sadistically at the assistant. "The police are on their way."

The assistant's colour drained, and he removed the bag and its contents from the counter, and put them down on the floor.

In the meantime, Joe spoke with Tanner and from the outset, it was not a pleasant conversation.

"I don't think I have anything to say to you, Murray."

"Good. Because I have something to say to you. I think I've found your camera."

"You're not listening to me. When I tell you…" A long silence followed. "Say that again."

"You heard me, you idiot. I'm in a second-hand shop in Penzance, and I need the serial number of your camera so that I can confirm that the one they are holding is yours. You do have the serial number with you?"

"Why would I have the serial number with me?"

"Because you're that kind of pain in the posterior." Joe chewed his lip. "I don't suppose you have it stored online, do you?"

"Well, I might have."

"Okay, here's what you do. See if you can find the number and then text it to me. Also, text me details of what we might find in the bag; the number of lenses and any other stuff. I'm waiting for the police to turn up at the shop and I won't be leaving until I've seen them."

"All right. Very good. I'll do that."

Joe killed the call, and stared the assistant in the eye. "It looks like we have a good few minutes to wait, son."

The young man again scratched his beard. "I accepted it. I paid her for it, and she showed me documents proving it was hers. She'd bought it from a genuine dealer in Camborne."

"I can print that kind of document for fun on my computer at home."

A few minutes passed before Joe's phone bleeped to indicate an incoming message. He opened the screen, and accessed the latest text from Tanner. Leaving it on screen, he spoke again to the assistant. "Do you wanna get the camera out, so I can check the serial number on the body?"

It took considerably less than a minute to confirm that the camera was, indeed, Les Tanner's, and as if the serial number was not enough to confirm it, Tanner's list indicated two lenses, a lens hood, and a bottle of lens polish and cloth, all of which they found in the bag. In the space of those few moments, Joe's fury rose as everything became clear to him, not least the way Brenda had called it right while he had got everything so horribly wrong.

When Hattie O'Neill arrived, the assistant was talking to his head office. As she inspected the camera, confirming Joe's findings, he terminated the phone call, and said, "I'm told I have to shut the doors for the day. Head office is sending a team down to take stock, and check on how many more pieces we have that might be stolen."

Hattie, who had been wearing forensic gloves throughout the exchange, insisted he pack the camera back into its case, and drop it into a large evidence bag, which she sealed and labelled. "When he gets here, tell your boss to ring me and I will furnish you with a list of all items we know to be stolen in this area." She turned and smiled at Joe. "Well done. It looks like you might have cleared up a problem for us."

"And I'm not done yet. Can you get your loudmouth boss to Gittings?"

"Sure, but I don't think he'll be interested in theft on this kind of scale."

"Maybe not. But if you can get him there, I'll give you and him Winnie Kalinowski's killer."

It was a measure of the trust she put in him that she made

the necessary phone call, and promised Joe, "He'll be there at three o'clock. But I'm warning you, he's not pleased. We're still interrogating Tolley and Ambrose."

Joe smiled broadly. "There's only one thing I like as much as handing over a killer, and that's showing a smartarsed cop the error of his ways."

Chapter Eighteen

Hattie was right. Howell was in an appalling frame of mind when he entered Joe's caravan just after three in the afternoon.

Joe did not rush back to Gittings. After letting Tanner know that the camera was, indeed, his, he enjoyed a leisurely stroll around the centre of Penzance, bought a couple of toys for young Danny, and more souvenirs for Cheryl and Lee, and another map of Arthurian Cornwall, this time for the wall of his flat. When he was finished shopping, he took an early, but equally relaxed lunch alone in the shopping mall, made his way back to the car, and then drove steadily to Hayle, where he handed the rental car in. After completing the necessary administration, he took a taxi to Gittings, deliberately avoided the show bar and entertainment centre, where he knew most of the 3rd Age Club would be gathered, and went straight to his caravan.

He had intended a word with Brenda, but she was not there. A quick call to Alec Staines, and he learned that she had gone to St Ives for the day with Stewart Dalmer.

He was not worried about it. He was confident that Tanner would have telephoned and told her of developments, and whatever he and she needed to say could be dealt with later in the day, preferably when they were alone.

The anger which had consumed him for the last few days was reminiscent of that which had driven him from Palmanova, with the possible exception that fleeing Majorca was also spurred by a large dose of fear. With the recollection of a significant incident from the previous night, the same could be said of Gittings, except that the tremors were retrospective, and only entered his consciousness when he realised what had been going on. He had had a lucky escape, and what had seemed like an inconsequential, drunken incident at the time, took on a new significance. At that point, the events of the entire week passed through some kind of space warp in his mind, and came out with a different focus, the one his suspicions should have been targeting all week.

Worse than the anger was the feeling of foolishness. He had always prided himself on his discernment, his ability to evaluate, assess people and come to accurate conclusions. Over the last five days or more, he could not have been further off the mark if he had turned his back and aimed his assessments in the opposite direction. He had been made to look a fool, and that hurt. He could not, however, place the blame anywhere but upon himself, and he was determined that the assault on his self-respect would not go unpunished.

But first he had to deal with Howell and Hattie.

"I hope you know what you're talking about, Murray. We already have our main suspects in custody, and one or other of them will eventually crack."

"If you'll take some advice, Howell, you'd be better releasing them," Joe replied tartly. "You have the wrong men. In fact, you should not be looking for men at all, but a man and a woman."

"The bruises on her neck, pal. I told you, they match Tolley's dabs."

"Yes, but that's not what killed her, is it? You told me that three days ago. She was stabbed with a bread knife. Tolley admitted to having a row with her, and putting his hands round her throat?"

"You know he did. I told you that the other day, too."

"Yeah, well, that's all he did. Get Eleanor Dorning, and let's go to her caravan, and while you're at it, send a couple of your people in to bring Charlie Curnow. I'll explain everything when we get there."

Howell was still doubtful, but Hattie was already on her way through the door.

Joe and the inspector followed at a more leisurely pace, and as they made their way along the lines of vans, Joe explained his deductions.

"Right from the outset, we went about this from the wrong angle. We assumed that Winnie had been killed by either Tolley or Ambrose; the one to avoid her revealing his alleged drug dealing, and the other because he was besotted and didn't want anyone else to have her. We also looked at Charlie Curnow, because she threatened him on the day we arrived, and it would have been logical enough. But there was more going here than sex between the staff, drug dealing – if, in fact, there is any drug dealing – and selling contraband tobacco. Hattie told me that Gittings, in common with many other sites in the area, has been the focus of thefts throughout the season, and Winnie's mother told me that her daughter was involved. You're an experienced copper, you know that when thieves are at work, they need to fence the goods. When I found Les Tanner's camera this morning, everything slotted into place. I knew exactly what was going on, who organised it, and that, coupled to something last night, something I never gave another thought to, told me who killed Winnie. The one thing we were right about was the reason Winnie was killed. She knew too much for her own good."

When they reached the staff accommodation, they found Hattie and a concerned Eleanor waiting for them. The park manager greeted them worriedly. "Will someone tell me what's going on?"

Joe gave her a reassuring smile. "Yeah, no problem, Eleanor. Once we get inside." He gestured at the door, inviting her to unlock it.

They stepped into the caravan. The police officers stood back to cover the door, Joe leaned on the worktop by the sink, and Eleanor faced them from the centre of the room.

"This is my downtime. I'm not due on duty again until four o'clock, so will you please tell me what is the matter?"

Joe again took centre stage. "Simple enough. It's about you arranging the murder of Winnie Kalinowski after she threatened to expose your trade in stolen goods."

Her colour drained. Shock shot across her face, followed

quickly by fury. "What? Have you taken leave of your senses?"

"No. I've just come to them. This morning, as a matter of fact."

It seemed impossible for her eyes to widen further, but they did. "You have, haven't you? You've lost the plot."

Joe ignored the jibe. "There are a number of things that didn't ring quite true about you, but you managed to bury my curiosity. And we both know how, don't we?" He left the rhetorical question hanging, and pressed on with his verbal assault. "You told me you were on split shifts this week because it was your turn. Quite honestly, I thought it was odd for a senior manager to work splits at all, but then one of the entertainment crew let slip that it wasn't just this week. It's every week. You prefer it that way. But still it didn't occur to me why. I saw you in the car park on Wednesday in Penzance, with an empty shopping bag. When I asked on Wednesday night, you said you were looking for an iPad. Truth is, you weren't looking for anything. I was in that second-hand shop, Entiex, this morning, and even then, I didn't make the connection, and I might never have done had it not been for a coincidence. When I went into the shop, I spotted a camera, the very camera Les Tanner had stolen. You sold them that camera on Wednesday."

Eleanor remained defiant. "I don't know what you're talking about."

"Yes, well, if I get it wrong, I'm sure Inspector Howell will let me know. But I'm willing to bet that if the cops check your laptop, or the one I'm sure you have at your house in Truro, they'll come across a document proving that the camera was owned by Linda Trelawney, but we know it was owned by Les Tanner. He's a pain in the buttock, Les. He works for the local council, and he has this annoying habit of keeping stupid things in cloud storage. Things like serial numbers of his technology equipment, which includes his thousand-pound camera. It was definitely his, and the real reason you were in Penzance on Wednesday was to sell it. And before you deny it any further, I'm sure the assistant will remember you."

Eleanor shrugged. "Even if you're right, and I'm not saying you are, what does that have to do with Wynette's murder?"

"Nothing. But that's because you didn't do it. Your partner did."

Eleanor snorted. "What partner? I don't have any partners. Business or personal."

Joe did not answer. The sound of a scuffle from outside prevented him.

Howell and Hattie stood away from the door, as it flew open, and Charlie Curnow, manhandled by two uniformed officers, burst into the caravan. Howell closed the door again, and stood in front of it, barring the way out.

Curnow ended up in the middle of the room, alongside Eleanor, the uniforms either side of them. His podgy face was a mask of fury.

"What the hell is going on? I have work to do."

"It's all over, Charlie," Joe said. "The only work you'll be doing from now on is in the prison laundry."

"What are you—"

Joe cut him off. "You know your trouble? You live in the past, and this time, it was your undoing, but I didn't realise it until a few hours ago. You can't help bragging about your past glories, can you, Charlie?" Joe deliberately goaded him. "'Oh I was on the telly, you know, and I was in the Royal Marines before they booted me out'. You just couldn't help telling me, could you? And then I suddenly twigged everything, and it prompted a memory from my past. A feature film from the nineteen-fifties, and the way in which commandos were taught to silently kill. A knife under the rib cage, driven upwards to pierce the heart. Just the way Wynette Kalinowski was killed."

Charlie's features were manic. "Have you taken leave of your senses, or do you make a habit of talking out of your backside?"

"Well, you're right to an extent," Joe agreed. "And even if I thought about it earlier, it wouldn't have been conclusive...

if you hadn't tried to run me down when I left this van last night." Curnow was about to protest, but Joe did not give him the chance. "Even then, I could have overlooked it by assuming you were drunk. In fact, I did. It's only when I put the two together, that I added two and two and finally got four."

Joe began to speak to the van's occupants in general.

"Here's the way I see it. When Charlie stumbled in here the other night, he put on a convincing act of being drunk, but the truth is, he thought I'd left, and he was coming here for an update on whatever progress I'd made, or for his bit of fun in Eleanor's bed. It doesn't really matter which, the point is, it was not a mistake coming here as he tried to claim. It was intentional. Not only that, but it was vital because they had to know what I knew. These two," Joe waved a hand at the pair, "are the major fences for all stolen items from the local holiday parks. Curnow already had contacts. He told me as much when he admitted bootlegging booze and tobacco. So I reckon that a good proportion of the stolen goods are sold to foreign sailors, crew men and women on the cargo and passenger boats which put into Penzance, Falmouth, and Cornwall's other ports. Eleanor does her part by selling them on to second-hand dealers in the area, which, incidentally is probably the real reason you were in Truro, the same day as Stewart Dalmer. Wynette was part of this gang, and her mother was putting pressure on her to give it up, find an honest living. She was ambitious, that girl. She wanted more than putting on turns for happy campers on a crummy holiday park. Not one of the entertainments staff had a good word to say about her, but I reckon that was just professional jealousy. All right, she didn't have the sweetest voice I've ever heard, but she had experience, and she could probably make something more of herself. So she wanted out, but also wanted cash, and that's the proposition she put to Eleanor, Curnow, maybe even Flick and Quint. Pay up and I'll shut up. I think you'll find, Inspector, that Flick and Quint were not party to the final decision. It was these two. They needed to shuffle that poor girl off. I think Eleanor arranged to meet her in the dunes, but Curnow was the one wielding the knife."

Eleanor sneered again. "Prove it."

"I don't have to." Joe turned his back on them, tore off a sheet of kitchen towel, reached into the drawer and took out the breadknife he had been so reluctant to use during the week. As he held it up for them all to see, he wondered whether his subconscious had been trying to telegraph the truth to him. "If you check this over, Howell, you may yet find traces of Winnie on it."

Hattie held forward an evidence bag and Joe dropped the implement in.

He turned on Eleanor. "It doesn't matter how well you cleaned it, there'll be microscopic traces, and if you haven't touched it since, I'm certain they'll find Charlie's dabs all over it. How will you explain that?"

There was a momentary silence and then, without warning, Charlie hurled himself at Joe. He had taken barely two paces before the uniformed constables restrained him.

Eleanor glowered at Joe, and her voice was a hiss of pure hatred. "Do you know what a despicable little man you are?"

Joe laughed by return. "Water off a duck's back. If you wanna get under my skin, try criticising my steak and kidney pudding."

Chapter Nineteen

Brenda found Joe right where she expected. She had returned to their shared caravan to shower and change for the evening, and learned that he had already gone out. He did not answer his phone and a few calls to others elicited no clue as to his whereabouts.

An uncharacteristically diffident and apologetic Les Tanner worried that he might have decided to sever all ties with them, but Brenda knew different. A fifty-year insight into the man told her exactly where to look, and when she was ready she made her way up the lane to the crest of the hill, where she found him sitting on a grassy hummock, squatting, tailor fashion, legs crossed, his digital camera in hand, looking out over the beach and sea beyond, watching the sun as it dipped towards the horizon.

This, she knew, was going to be difficult.

She sat down alongside him, disregarding the sand which would inevitably cover her trousers. "All right?"

He puffed on a hand-rolled cigarette, and gestured at the setting sun. "We came here the first evening, remember? You and me, Les and Sylvia. Les was bragging about his new camera."

"The one that was stolen and which you got back… Well, which he'll eventually get back when the police are done prosecuting Eleanor Dorning and Charlie Curnow."

Joe grunted and kept his eyes on the sun.

Brenda took a deep breath. "I was out of order yesterday. I know I hurt you, Joe, and I had no right to say those things to you."

He shrugged and raised his camera, and kept an eye on the tiny screen. The sun was flattening out into an oblate sphere as it neared the horizon. When he was happy that the camera was steady, the image as he wanted it, the resolution adequate, he pressed the shutter, and then examined the finished product.

Happy with it, he turned his head to face Brenda. "You were saying?"

Her irritation began to rise. "Don't make this any more difficult than it is, Joe. I'm trying to say I'm sorry."

"Why? Everything you said was dead right. You were just obeying the old Sanfordian rule of telling it like it is."

He sighed, stubbed out his cigarette, and began to roll a fresh one. He had to pause halfway through the process to take another picture of the sun as the horizon cut it in half. When he was happy with it, he returned to rolling a cigarette, and once that was completed, he lit up and took a deep drag.

"The trouble with you and Sheila is you're too smart for your own good. You know me better than I know myself. I've been running away, Brenda. Ever since Denise was killed. I was happy with her. Happy working at The Lazy Luncheonette, happy to help with her investigations, happy to have you two, Lee, Cheryl, and the part-timers working with me. Happy to see the draymen every morning. From my point of view, I had it made. And then that crazy so-and-so ran her off the road and killed her, and that ripped the heart right out of my life."

Brenda sympathised. "I've been there, Joe. When Colin died. I know what you went through."

She knew that he had heard, that he had listened, but it was as if she had said nothing. "Then there was that business in Palmanova. I ran away from that too. I think anyone would have legged it under those circumstances. How long was I gone? Three, four months? That crazy bitch made me fear for my life, and it began to dawn on me that I'm not immortal." He tapped his temple. "One day, this mind will cease to function, and Joe Murray will be no more. It's a scary thought. I think you and Sheila had already dealt with it, when you lost your husbands. I lost the old man, the old lady, but it still didn't get through to me. So when I eventually came back after Palmanova, I was determined to look after number one, get some enjoyment out of life before I meet the Grim Reaper. And while I was out there, busy chasing women, generally having a good time, I forgot the people who should matter most: Lee and Cheryl, little Danny, you and Sheila, and our other friends, the folk we've known for fifty odd years." He took another drag on his smoke and shook his head. "You were angry last night, but you weren't out of order. You were bang on the mark."

Brenda took a few moments to take in this unusual image of a reflective Joe, and while she was busy mulling over his words, he took several more pictures of the sun, the final one just as a last bead of crimson disappeared into the haze.

In an effort to side-track the discussion, she asked, "Have the police nailed Dorning and Curnow?"

Joe nodded. "Hattie rang me an hour ago. First thing they did was search her house in Truro, they found tons of stuff from their list of stolen goodies. And guess what. They even found Winnie Kalinowski's mobile phone there. The barefaced sods not only murdered the poor girl, but they robbed her, as well."

Brenda nodded sagely. "It sounds pretty conclusive."

Joe was more confident. "Finding the phone makes it practically certain that one or other of them murdered her, and my money is still on Curnow. The charge against him will have to wait until they get a forensic analysis of the breadknife, but he did it. I'll stake next year's profits on it." He tutted irritably. "And as for her… well, she gave me a good time this week, but what was she really doing? Keeping tabs on what I'd learned. That's what." Now he laughed, but without humour. "Maybe my reputation got here ahead of me."

"Your reputation as a detective or a lover?"

There was more pleasure in Joe's laughter this time. "Both."

With their last fling in mind, Brenda could see the discussion was heading into troublesome areas, and sought to redirect it again. "Les is ready to apologise for making a complaint against you." She gave a nervy little chuckle. "Let's face it, he doesn't have much choice, does he? Not after you found his camera."

"He's a careless idiot. Maybe it'll teach him not to leave it lying around in caravans in future."

"He's learned a few lessons this week." Brenda took another deep breath. "He's resigning the Chair come the New Year."

Although Joe had never been informed, it was not entirely unexpected. Since Tanner took over on a permanent basis, during Joe's extended absence after the visit to Palmanova, he had not proved popular with the members. He was too officious, too pernickety, too busy crossing t's and dotting i's to get on with the things which were important to the membership. And he lacked Joe's negotiating skills. Indeed, although Joe no longer held an official position within the club, they had continued to rely on him to grind down the price on excursions. Gittings was a case in point. Those members who had attended the relevant meetings had voted for it, Tanner had rubberstamped the decision, but he asked Joe to speak to Gittings and get the price down as far as he could.

However, in Joe's opinion – and he had never been slow to express it – Tanner's management style was too autocratic, too hands on. He tried to run the 3rd Age Club along the same lines as he ran Sanford Borough Council's Payroll Department at the town hall, and it grated on the members.

He replied to Brenda's observation. "So who's next in line?"

"Stewart."

Joe sneered. "Dalmer? Will he have time between chasing antique fairs all over the North and Midlands? He'd be a rubbish choice. Elect him, and the club's next outing will be to the *Antiques Roadshow*." He gave her a wistful smile. "I'm not having a go at him personally, Brenda. I know you've been getting it on with him this week, and it's none of my business, but I'm thinking of the club."

Brenda felt a rush of love for him. This was more like the

old Joe, the Joe she had known since their school days. "You don't know how pleased I am to hear that, Joe. You have to get back on board. Stand for the Chair. For all Les's complaints about your haphazard administration, you knew what you were doing, and you never did it for yourself." She began to urge him. "We don't want Stewart in the Chair. We need you back where you were, where you belong. Please, Joe."

He smiled at her. "You don't want Stewart in the Chair? You want him all to yourself?"

"Bog off. You know what I mean."

He yawned. "It's been a bad week."

Despite the apparent irrelevance of the comment, Brenda responded. "Oh, I don't know. The weather's been good, and the excursions were spot on. And you can hardly complain. You had her well-saddled before you handed her over to plod."

"You didn't do so bad yourself judging by the way the van was rocking on its suspension." Before she could respond, he pressed on. "No, that's not what I meant when I said it's been bad. It's what I was trying to say before you told me Les was resigning. I have this occasional thing with Maddy back home, but it's not going anywhere. It never will, and if she never saw me again, I shouldn't think she'd lose any sleep. And I just said, didn't I, that Eleanor was using me. All right so I got a bit of the other – a lot of the other, to be truthful – but she was keeping tabs on me. She's not the first either. I'm tempted to say Alison did the same thing when she married me, but at least she stuck around for ten years. You're right, Brenda. My place is with real people, my people, and I should be in the Chair of the Sanford 3rd Age Club. When's the vote?"

"End of January."

Joe racked his mind for the articles of the 3rd Age Club. "So nominations close at the end of October."

"You've a month, Joe. You'll need a proposer and a seconder. I'm sure George and Owen will oblige. You'll also need twelve signatures in support. You're guaranteed mine,

Sheila's, Alec and Julia Staines, and Les is not keen on Stewart, so I'm sure he'll support you, and so will Sylvia. That's six for starters. Mort Norris and his missus don't like Stewart, and I'm sure Cyril Peck and Mavis Barker will vote for you. It won't take much to get the Pyecocks to back you. That's the twelve you need." Her eyes burned into him. "But don't do it out of a sense of obligation, Joe. You have to mean it. Do it because you want to."

He got to his feet, held out a hand and helped Brenda up. They turned and made their way slowly back to their shared caravan.

"I'll speak to Les tonight, and if he's definitely standing down, I'll announce it on the bus tomorrow morning."

Brenda stopped, turned, smiled on him, and kissed him on the cheek. "I can't wait for you to tell the world that Joe Murray is back onside."

***

At a quarter past eight on Saturday morning, Keith negotiated the large roundabout North of Hayle, and picked up the A30.

"Another four hundred miles, give or take, and we'll be home."

Sat alongside Brenda, one row behind and across the aisle from Keith, Joe grunted his thanks. On reflection, he was glad to see the back of Cornwall in general, Gittings in particular, and although he had some memories to treasure, his dalliance with Eleanor Dorning, was not amongst them.

He had spoken with Les Tanner the previous evening in the show bar, and the captain confirmed that he was resigning, while expressing his apprehension at Dalmer's nomination. Along with many of the members, Tanner did not believe Dalmer was the right man to take them forward. When Joe told him he would stand against Dalmer, Tanner declared Joe to be a waste of time.

"But I can confirm you'll get my vote, Murray," he said with a wink and a wry smile.

As the bus laboured up the hill from the Loggan Moor roundabout, Joe got to his feet, reached past Brenda and took down the PA microphone.

"All right, people, there will be a couple of stops on the way, but we should still be home sometime this side of seven o'clock tonight. Now, in case you're wondering what I'm doing holding the microphone, rather than your Chairman, it's because, as you've all been made aware, there'll be a vote for the Chair in the New Year. Stewart, I'm not having a go at you, but I'm telling you all right now, so we can squash any rumours before they start, that I will be standing in that election. That's all. Enjoy the journey home."

The news was greeted with a smattering of applause, and it was left to George Robson to summarise.

"Welcome back, Joe. Anything for free beer."

THE END

The STAC Mystery series:
#1 The Filey Connection
#2 The I-Spy Murders
#3 A Halloween Homicide
#4 A Murder for Christmas
#5 Murder at the Murder Mystery Weekend
#6 My Deadly Valentine
#7 The Chocolate Egg Murders
#8 The Summer Wedding Murder
#9 Costa del Murder
#10 Christmas Crackers
#11 Death in Distribution
#12 A Killing in the Family
#13 A Theatrical Murder
#14 Trial by Fire
#15 Peril in Palmanova
#16 The Squire's Lodge Murders
#17 Murder at the Treasure Hunt
#18 A Cornish Killing

Fantastic Books
Great Authors

darkstroke is
an imprint of
Crooked Cat Books

- Gripping Thrillers
- Cosy Mysteries
- Romantic Chick-Lit
- Fascinating Historicals
- Exciting Fantasy
- Young Adult and Children's Adventures
- Non-Fiction

Discover us online
www.darkstroke.com

Find us on instagram:
www.instagram.com/darkstrokebooks

Printed in Great Britain
by Amazon